DEAD LINE

by

Colin McAlpin

Eloquent Books
New York, New York

Copyright 2009
All rights reserved – Colin McAlpin

No part of this book may be reproduced or transmitted in any form
or by any means, graphic, electronic, or mechanical, including
photocopying, recording, taping, or by any information storage
retrieval system, without the permission, in writing, from the
publisher.

Eloquent Books
An imprint of AEG Publishing Group
845 Third Avenue, 6th Floor - 6016
New York, NY 10022
www.eloquentbooks.com

ISBN: 978-1-60860-780-8

Printed in the United States of America

Book Design: SP

To Scarlett.

TABLE OF CONTENTS

PROLGUE...7

ONE.. 11
TWO.. 15
THREE...21
FOUR..27
FIVE..31
SIX..45
SEVEN..53
EIGHT...67
NINE...83
TEN...91
ELEVEN..97
TWELVE.. 105
THIRTEEN.. 115
FOURTEEN...123
FIFTEEN...135
SIXTEEN...141
SEVENTEEN... 157
EIGHTEEN..167
NINETEEN..175
TWENTY.. 189
TWENTY-ONE...193
TWENTY-TWO..203

PROLOGUE

PEGGY Sue was getting married. Her name wasn't really Peggy Sue but that's how Rachel thought of her. Her real name was Roberta Wazowski, but Rachel got it into her head that it was Peggy Sue. The thought stuck with her.

It should have been something hippie like Moonbeam or Sunflower but it was Roberta ... or Peggy Sue.

She was 24-years-old, pushing 16. She was as thin as a bamboo cane – she'd prefer it if you described her as willowy – and she was dressed in an ankle-length 1960's Flower Power dress. Her red hair was frizzy and cascaded Raphaelite down to her shoulders, around which was draped a brightly-patterned purple beaded shawl. Very of-the-period. It wasn't, though, this period.

She was a gloriously colourful throwback to the faraway days of making love not war, of roses in rifle barrels, of protests against everything.

She really was getting married. That much was certain, was written in the stars. Rachel knew she was getting married because Roberta-Peggy Sue-Moonbeam-Sunflower had spent the best part of 45 minutes telling her all about it and all about Jack – who was, apparently, just about the grooviest guy you could ever meet and destined for great things in his uncle Herbie's auto repair shop – and all about the approaching ceremony and about the absolutely awesome dress she and her mom, who was divorced from her pop, but they were both civilised people and were coming to the wedding, had picked out earlier that day in Yours Nuptially in Manhattan and about the honeymoon at Niagara Falls, which were awesome even if it left you with the nagging thought that you'd left the bath running, and about the absolutely awesome house they had managed to absolutely, awesomely steal in Croton-Harmon and about ... well, about everything else that was groovy and absolute and awesome.

All of this relentless tide of information had hit Rachel like a Pacific roller from the moment she had taken a seat in the Lounge Car of Amtrak's Lake Shore Limited out of Penn Station. Rachel had selected the empty table because she needed to sort out the pages of notes she had made on her trip to New York. She got as far as flicking open her notebook and plucking the top off her ball-pen and then Hurricane Roberta-whatever struck with its devastating force.

As the train creaked and groaned its way slowly, if hardly awesomely, through the Manhattan suburbs towards the wide Hudson River, Rachel and everyone else in the Lounge Car heard about the life and absolutely awesome times of Roberta-whatever.

The initial introduction had come before the train had even begun its journey from the famous 7th Avenue and 32nd Street station when Roberta-whatever set a collection of shopping bags on the table, slid into the seat opposite and immediately informed Rachel that she could tell instantly that she was a Cancerian. It was a gift. It never failed. Worked every time. First go. Bang!

"Pardon?" Rachel said, extracting her crumpled notebook from beneath one of the bags and taking in the explosion of colour across the table.

"Cancer," the explosion repeated, "I'm Roberta Wazowski ... and your star sign is Cancer. I can tell."

"I'm Rachel Andrews," Rachel said and offered her hand across the forest of shopping, "and I'm not ..."

"No," Roberta held up both hands, "don't tell me, I just know what you are ... of course, you're Gemin ..."

Rachel shook her head: "No. I'm Piscean: born March second."

"I knew it, didn't I say it was a gift?" Roberta cried in triumph, "I had you figured for Pisces. And you're Scotch, I can tell that as well. You're Scotch."

Rachel ran the quick thought through her head that at that exact moment she wished she were. A strong Scotch had a lot going for it at that exact moment.

"Well, actually I'm Irish, Northern Irish ... from Belfast. And it's Scots. The people are Scots and the drink is Scotch."

"I knew it, didn't I say you were Irish?"

Oh God! Why me? Maybe the train will suddenly derail and tumble down an embankment in flames and belching black smoke and twisted metal and screaming passengers and rescue me from this mad New York bag lady.

And as Roberta began the story of her life and her coming marriage, Rachel thought of her as Peggy Sue.

ONE

THEY were the golden couple. If you picked up a copy of the day's Denver Post or 5280 magazine and turned to the society pages, chances were that you'd find Jackson Wellman and the beautiful Delta Dubette-Wellman photographed at a glitterati arts or charity benefit. Indeed, the chances were they had funded the event with a hefty cheque.

The Colorado Symphony, The Denver Art Museum, the Colorado Ballet, the Denver Center for the Performing Arts, a new bursary for the University of Colorado at Boulder, a hospital wing here, a children's home there … you could always count on Jackson Wellman and Delta Dubette-Wellman to provide the necessary cheque by return of post, with a lavish fund-raising dinner-dance and at least several Senators and a couple of A List Hollywood stars thrown in to garner the headlines.

They were not merely members of Colorado society, they WERE Colorado society. Around them swirled all that was glamorous and exciting and generous and whenever you opened a copy of the Denver Post and 5280 there they would be, arm-in-arm and smiling: American Royalty.

Delta controlled 70% of Octagon Enterprises, having inherited the all-embracing company from her late father, Senator Bourke 'Bull' Dubette, who had come to Colorado in the 1920's as a young man eager to make his mark and his fortune. Whatever it took to achieve those twin ambitions, he did.

He had come up from Georgia, claiming, with passing but pointed modesty, that he sprang from the Savannah Dubettes, though a careful search for the distinguished family would not have yielded one iota of substantiation.

Not that it mattered since 'Bull' found Colorado to be the perfect place for a rollicking, enterprising young go-getter. And the world can forgive anything if anything and everything is brought to its doorstep by a rollicking young go-getter.

Delta, his only daughter, might well have genuinely come from the Old South. If you worked in central casting in Hollywood and hollered for a Southern Belle the minions would have brought you Delta. And you would have been delighted. She had been born in Denver, but she was more Southern Confederate than Scarlett O'Hara.

She was tall – 5ft 11ins – and she had flowing flame-coloured hair that tumbled around her shoulders. She had the sort of figure that entire regiments of Yankees and Rebels would happily have shed blood for. She had a peaches-and-cream complexion and a face that had you whistling Dixie.

She had been educated – detractors, behind her back, said it had been beyond her intelligence, though they still took the Dubette cheques – at various New England and Swiss colleges and had returned in the full bloom of her early twenties to Denver, to break hearts and cause devastation among the male elite of Colorado families.

Jackson Wellman was more of a rough diamond. He was a handsomely-tanned all-American Californian, from Orange County, and had landed in Colorado as a gunnery instructor at the United States Air Force Academy south of Denver.

When he left the Academy he found employment in one of the many companies owned by Octagon Enterprises. He worked hard and in time became one of a handful of middle-management gofers to 'Bull' Dubette. He was ambitious, though he never quite found the proper opening to exploit. He was content to bide his time and await his moment.

It came when he was invited to a Symphony concert – against his better judgement, since his musical tastes extended no further than the Beach Boys – and there he met Delta. He had never met her before, even though he worked for her father, but had seen her often enough in newspapers and magazines. The photographs did not come near to doing her justice.

She was … well, she was just beautiful. Nothing more required to be added.

They became an item and when he had proposed and been accepted, Delta took him on as her Special Project.

She persuaded 'Bull' to move Jackson up the Octagon food-chain. 'Bull', who until Delta had started dating him had scarcely noticed Jackson, gave him the struggling Octagon Publishing off-shoot to play around with. At least, 'Bull' figured, the title of Executive Publisher would please Delta and the business was in such a mess anyway that Jackson could hardly make things worse.

Octagon Publishing produced a handful of under-achieving specialist magazines that had ideas clearly above their stations: International Light Engineering, World Pharmaceuticals Digest, Global Aerodynamics Monthly. None of them sold collectively enough copies to fill a plastic shopping bag.

But, to everyone's amazement, Jackson grabbed the ailing patient by the throat and shook it into life. He modernised, he re-designed, he tweaked, he appointed young and talented editors and writers, and he let them get on with it. While they were getting on with it, he sought fresh openings and quickly launched new magazines for the film industry, for doctors, for railroad enthusiasts, for DIYers and branched out into in-house magazines for several large corporations, insurance companies and banks. Three weekly newspapers – in Colorado, Arizona and Utah - were also started.

Octagon Publishing became the glittering gem in the OE crown.

And then 'Bull' died. It was announced as a tragic heart attack by the Octagon Enterprises Press and Marketing Department, while Senator Dubette was conducting important Colorado business in Washington. What he was actually conducting in Washington was an over-energetic humping of a pretty young researcher in a motel room. 'Bull' would almost certainly have preferred the true story of his passing to have been revealed, but the proprieties had to be observed.

The subsequent will left the bulk of Octagon Enterprises shares to Delta. Until then, she had seldom visited any of the OE establishments, preferring her well-established lifestyle as one of Colorado's ladies who lunch and shop and sit on arts and charity committees and get their photographs in the newspapers and magazines. She had no inclination to change this arrangement.

She gave Jackson 15% of the shares, the rest being distributed around obscure and unproductive cronies of 'Bull', and he took over the complete command of OE.

And the business grew and expanded even more. It was said that you could not eat, wear, drive, read, play or otherwise use anything in Colorado, Wyoming, Utah, Arizona, Nebraska and New Mexico that wasn't manufactured or supplied by Octagon Enterprises.

Jackson and Delta, who had never found the time to produce children, moved into 'Bull's' house in the quaint little Rockies vacation town of Estes Park. So famous was the large, two-storey, white-painted, eight-bedroom house that sat on a hill – its very own hill, no less - looking down on the town, that it was known to all simply as The Hall.

It became the focal point for the glitterati. Everyone who was, or thought themselves to be, of consequence fretted and fought over invitations to The Hall. Parties at The Hall were legendary, dances formidable, mere cups of coffee cherished moments of personal pride and achievement.

Estes Park, The Gutsiest Little Town in Colorado, was known as the Gateway to the Rockie Mountains and The Hall, for those fortunate to be invited, became the Gateway to Colorado Society.

They were the golden couple, with a marriage made in Heaven. They were a team, always smiling, always the perfect hosts, the perfect … but, then again, ask yourself, how perfect can perfection be?

TWO

APRIL had turned into a nothing month. There was a faint half-promise of Spring in the still chilled air but the days failed to live up to even that expectation and instead delivered rain. It didn't come as Those April Showers but in depressing downpours that bounced off the pavements and cut to the bone.

Rachel Andrews parked her Citroen in the car park behind the Movie House on the Dublin Road, gathered her notebook and pushed it into the black shoulder-bag that contained her laptop. She got out and, pulling the collar of her raincoat up around her ears and holding the bag over her head as a makeshift umbrella, ran through the puddles to the front door of the News Letter office at Metro Building on Donegall Square South.

She smiled a greeting to Kim on the reception desk and took off her coat. She carried it into the News Room, where she hung it, still dripping, on a wire hanger.

It was 9.30 in the morning and only a handful of her fellow reporters were at their desks. She walked through the News Room and sat down at her desk. Opposite her, her friend Brian Leonard, with whom she had shared by-lines on several recent major stories, was talking on the telephone and scribbling furiously.

She mimed drinking a coffee and he nodded. She walked to the table against the wall and flicked on the electric kettle. She spooned coffee and sugar into two mugs and when the water had bubbled hot she poured it into the mugs, adding milk.

She returned to the desk just as Brian was finishing his conversation and handed a mug across to him.

"No wee buttered scones, then?" he asked.

"Nope. Didn't have time to stop off," she said, cupping the mug in her hands, "I wanted to finish the last filler for Wednesday's column. I'll treat you to a healthy plate of Joe's fish 'n' chips at lunchtime."

"Wow!" he said, "It's first class all the way with you, isn't it?"

"Live life at the far edges is my motto!"

"So, it's still pissing down outside, I see. Hope the famous Andrews legs didn't get too damp. If you need them rubbed you know I'm always here for you ... and them."

"Not in your lifetime," she laughed.

Rachel was 20, pretty, blonde, feisty, sharp as a pin and she loved working on the Belfast morning newspaper. The News Letter was one of the world's oldest newspapers; indeed, it held the proud distinction of being the newspaper with the longest-running unbroken publication in the English language, going all the way back to the late 1700's. Rachel sometimes reckoned a couple of the original staff still lurked in quiet corners, quill pens akimbo.

She had been a reporter for two-and-a-bit years and had earned her own twice-weekly column – Wednesdays and Saturdays – on the strength of a particularly gruesome series of murders that she and Brian had covered, and which had involved her personally.

Her contribution to those stories had brought her several tempting offers from the large Belfast evening newspaper, the Belfast Telegraph, and from Ulster Television but she had declined them both. She knew she still had a lot to learn – though she was learning it fast – and, besides, she loved the News Letter and the opportunity it had given her.

There would be plenty of time for moving on. But not quite yet.

"What's doing?" she asked Brian.

He shrugged: "Nothing exciting, just a follow-up to a story in one of the country 'papers, the Impartial Reporter in Enniskillen I think," he sifted through the pile of papers scattered across his desk, "yes, the Impartial. Seems a couple of farmers have been moving cattle back and forth across the border and claiming subsidies from the North and the Republic. Our beloved leader wanted it beefed up a bit – pardon the pun – with stats and fresh quotes."

"My, my!" Rachel said, with an elaborate yawn, "what an exciting story. Waken me when it's Easter!"

"By the by," Brian said, holding up a piece of paper, "the delectable Jayne called just before you trickled in ... she's in the office and can you call her back. She has an interesting proposition for you

… pity she never has one for me."

"You poor thing. I must mention that to your wife when next we have coffee and a gossip. Jayne's at the Beeb, you say?"

He nodded and she picked up the receiver.

Rachel and Jayne and Sandi had been close friends for many years, since school and university days. There had once been four of them, but Sarah had been one of the tragic victims of the previous year's serial killings. They still, though, called themselves the Gang of Four.

Jayne was a producer in the Ormeau Avenue headquarters of BBC Northern Ireland, just around the corner from the new offices of the newspaper, working specifically on documentaries for Radio Ulster. Sandi was a talented, much-sought-after silversmith with her own studio-workshop and a growing list of clients. They were as different and as alike as three friends could be.

Rachel waited for the Broadcasting House switchboard to find Jayne, wondering what the interesting proposition might be.

When her friend was eventually found, interesting it certainly proved to be.

"Now that's what I'd call interesting," Rachel said when the excited Jayne had outlined the pitch she had just given her boss, and just had accepted … with the usual non-committal, maybe, give or take, run it up the mast and see if the wheels stay on, yes and then again no provisos BBC bosses are notorious for.

This boss, like all BBC bosses, bafflingly appeared to be the SE of DPRU. None of this made any sense to Rachel but it seemed to be exciting news for Jayne.

"So what would you call interesting?" Brian wanted to know.

"Where to begin," Rachel said, "Well, you know at the BBC they hold regular meetings, the creative people and the ones who go only by obscure initials, and they held one last night. And Jayne has been putting together an idea for a six-part radio documentary, and she pitched it at the meeting and this Officer Commanding Interesting Programmes or something reckoned it was a runner."

"And?"

"And? Oh, what was Jayne's interesting proposition? Well, she suggested a series she's called Coast to Coast, a journey across America on Amtrak …"

"That's the United States' railway system …"

"The National Railroad Passenger Corporation to be exact.

Jayne's idea is to take the train from the East Coast, Boston, all the way across to San Diego on the West Coast.

"The Irish built the American railways and there's all those railway songs. She suggested a top personality could front the series, somebody like that popular Country singer, Crawford Bell, and talk to the crews running the trains, the passengers, stop off in some of the interesting places along the way, throw in a bit of history. She even thought a coffee-table book could be published alongside the series. It might even be turned into a television series with an accompanying radio series, plus the book."

"Sounds a winner," Brian said, "How would she go about setting it all up?"

"She reckons she'd have to make a preliminary journey herself, gather background, do research, make useful contacts … you know, that sort of thing. Of course, she'd have to pay for it herself, but she's willing to risk that, take it as a holiday."

"I'm beginning to see the bigger picture," Brian guessed, "You wouldn't want Jayne to do this all on her own, would you? She'd need somebody to carry her pensils … somebody who's petite and blonde. Well, bugger me … she'd need you along for the ride!"

"Got it in one!"

"It's a spooky knack."

"Well, just think: she's planning to do the research in June-July … Boston, Chicago, Denver, Salt Lake City, San Fransisco, Los Angeles, San Diego. I could lump all this year's holidays together, maybe even take some unpaid time off.

"I could take the trusty old laptop and send back a whole series of features, they'd be perfect for the Silly Season when there's nothing much else happening. Do you think the boss would go for it?"

"Actually it sounds a terrific idea: Andrews in America sort of thing. Get him in the right mood, flash the old legs, laugh uncontrollably at his jokes, a bit of cleavage … you're already on the first train."

"I'm getting excited about it already. You really think the Editor would go for it?"

"If you paid for the trip yourself."

"Yes, I know that. I can always put the bite on darling Karen. She's running out of Brownie Points."

"Better be careful or your zany step-mother will want to go with you. Remember what happened when she went with you, Jayne and

Sandi to Karpathos? But, knowing Karen, I don't think you'll have any trouble getting the sponsorship."

It was high fives all round when Rachel emerged from her meeting with the Editor. She sat down at her desk and beamed broadly at Brian.

"I take it he gave you the go-ahead," he said.

"You bet. He jumped at it."

"Must have been my good advice."

"Not entirely," she said, "I think my boundless talent played no small part. Anyway, I've talked him into a six-week trip …"

"Bloody hell! I'm lucky if he lets me sneak an extra half-hour for lunch."

"It's the legs, see … you just don't have the legs to pull it off."

"Yeah, OK! So when does the scam begin?"

"Have to work it out with Jayne, but the last couple of weeks in June, first two in July seems the most likely. And, of course, I'll have to sweet-talk darling Karen into a small emolument."

There were, Rachel had to admit, several strict conditions to her getting the time off. No fool he, the Editor had laid down the ground-rules:

At least two worthwhile stories/features/interviews per day.

At least one of the above stories//features/interviews to have a local – Northern Ireland – slant.

A twice-weekly Andrews in America running travelogue feature. This, in newspaper parlance, was referred to as The Big Read.

Her regular twice-weekly column to be maintained.

No more holidays/coffee-breaks/lunchtimes/free week-ends/etc/etc for the next ten years, at least.

The latter negotiable in the fullness of time.

"Well, finding a Northern Ireland angle in America shouldn't be too much of a problem," Brian said, "I mean, every time you turn a corner in an American city you're bumping into somebody from Ireland, aren't you?"

"We'll put our heads together," she said, "and come up with possible ideas. Like, for a just suppose, bring me the head of a Belfast-born cop now patrolling the mean streets of New York or Chicago. Or, a family from here who made it big there … or … I think there's a Brian Friel play on Broadway around then."

"Enough already," he protested, "I'll see what else I can come up with. The cop idea is actually quite good. Occasionally your two grey cells do manage to meet up and shake hands."

THREE

WENDY Brewer had a problem. She was 33, beautiful in a natural outdoors-sporty way; her pageboy-cut blonde hair and shapely, athletic, sun-tanned body begged to be reached out for and gently fingered.

And with her looks came brains. She had a Business Degree and a Marketing Degree from one of the more exclusive New England Ivy League establishments. The fact that she came from Boston and could call up, whenever it was required, a Cool Yankee Lady persona was also a bonus. English secretaries and PA's were famous as 'must have' office accessories, but failing an English Rose a New English Rose was certainly the next best thing.

Wendy Brewer was truly the next best thing, and then some.

She had, after graduating, moved West, climbed the corporate ladder and was now into her second well-paid year as Personal Assistant to her high-flying boss. She was on the fast-track, zooming ever upward, going places, shattering the glass ceiling.

She drove a sleek, red Mercedes convertable. She shopped in the most fashionably exclusive places for the most eye-catching of clothes, shoes, lingerie, handbags … you name it!

She lived in a two-bedroom apartment – bought and paid for – in a converted warehouse in a district of the city you needed a special password and a portfolio of references to get within a score of miles of.

She spent her vacations in Europe, at least two per year: England, Ireland, France, Italy, Greece. On a couple of occasions she decided not to travel too far and made do with two weeks in Mexico and one in Brazil. Oh yes, and she skied regularly in Aspen and was an accomplished horsewoman, a formidable tennis-player and, if all else failed, she could have made a decent living as a concert pianist.

She was squired around the best restaurants, parties, theatres and galleries by a constant stream of lantern-jawed and disgustingly wealthy men.

None of which was a problem.

She was having an affair with her high-flying boss. Her high-flying boss was Jackson Wellman of Octagon Enterprises.

And that was a problem.

They were, of course, discreet about it. In the tall, shaded-glass and brushed-steel Octagon House in Cleveland Place across from the Denver Civic Center Park, within reach of the Mile High city's 300-plus restaurants and restored historic district of Larimer Square – offering an additional 90 or so bars – in one of America's most beautiful places, they conducted their day-to-day meetings with brisk, even cool, efficiency. He, the boss; she, the dedicated assistant.

When they met in her apartment out towards Boulder, it was altogether another matter: a matter of passion and lust. And sex.

It had started sort-of innocently enough when Wendy had been working for Jackson for six or so months. She proved to be excellent at what she did. She worked hard, allowed the right people into his inner sanctum and kept away those with nothing to offer him and Octagon Enterprises. She accepted, on his and Delta's behalf, the invitations that would do them the most good. She worked independently of the OE PR people to ensure the most comprehensive and flattering of media attention. She even bought the many presents that Jackson gave to Delta, sent flowers and cards for important anniversaries, advised, praised, disagreed with and warned him against courses of action when it was needed.

It was joked, both inside and outside the offices of Octagon Enterprises, that Jackson was merely the figurehead and Wendy the real power. In a way, there was more than a grain of truth to this.

And her excellence was rewarded when Jackson was invited to Portland in Oregon to deliver a keynote speech to Pacific Northwestern magazine writers. He had asked Delta to accompany him but she said she had so many charity functions to help organise.

And, anyway, he was the one Portland magazine writers wanted to see and hear. And, anyway, meetings other than those concerning her many charities and arts organisations bored her to death.

Jackson was surprised his wife was even aware that Octagon

actually published magazines.

He turned to Wendy, inviting her to Portland on the grounds, which he genuinely felt when he made the suggestion, that she would be useful. Decorative, certainly.

She accepted, for the same reasons.

They flew from Denver International Airport in the company Lear and checked into the reserved adjoining rooms 200 and 202 in the downtown Hilton. The speech was to be delivered the following night so Jackson took Wendy for a tour of the City of Roses, culminating in a leisurely meal in one of the many fine restaurants.

As they strolled back to their hotel he felt... well, peculiar. Like a teenager on his first date with the High School queen. He had always been faithful to Delta, he acknowledged that he would not have achieved so much so quickly had it not been for Delta. Yet, there he was, walking beside the beautiful, talented, useful Wendy, feeling peculiar. He was not quite sure why he felt as he did.

At the door of her room, he politely thanked her for giving up her free time to come to a boring speech with him. She smiled warmly and assured him that for the salary she was paid the occasional boring speech was no great hardship. And they parted with a laugh.

Jackson found sleep difficult that night. He telephoned Delta – she was out at one of her meetings, of course – and left a message: he missed her, he loved her, etc., etc. He lay alone in the large bed and in the yellow glow of a high, full moon he found himself staring at the locked, connecting door between the rooms willing it to open, willing Wendy to come through it. Irrational, dangerous thoughts.

Early the following morning she did come to his room, but only to assist him with his coming speech and to approve the final draft that she made him read to her.

She returned to his room minutes before they were to join their hosts and the other guests to make sure he was "presentable" ... she flicked a straying strand of hair behind his right ear. She straightened his bow-tie, she plucked a small thread from the shoulder of his dinner-jacket.

And she pulled his face to hers and kissed him. It was a lingering, passionate kiss.

When the speech had been delivered and they had been tormented enough by the stream of well-wishers wanting to shake his hand and thank him for being such an inspirational speaker they hurried back to her room.

He watched her undress with tantalising slowness until she stood naked between his knees. She kneeled and he reached for her and drew her to him, kissing her breasts and burying his face in her stomach. She lay beside him on the bed and they made love: slowly, lovingly, passionately.

Their affair had started.

As it progress it grew in intensity and, he knew, danger. He knew there was so much he could lose, so much that he had worked so hard to make possible. Yet he could not, for all the terrible risks he was taking, stop. He was clinging onto a wildly surging roller-coaster, afraid of the moment when he would be flung from it.

He and Wendy went on business trips together, many of them invented for the sole purpose of helping them steal time together. He was always careful to ask Delta if she wanted to come, but he knew – hoped – she would apologise and cite yet another committee meeting. She almost always did.

There was, too, an element of tingling menace to their meetings. He would stay late in the office – to work, he would explain, on a new project – and Wendy would come to him. He would make love to her on his desk knowing that at any moment someone might discover them.

At the same time, he continued to be seen with Delta at all the right social events, to be photographed with Delta at this concert and that stage performance. For Jackson Wellman and Delta Dubette-Wellman were always the perfect, golden couple.

And, as all married men tend to while in the grip of a consuming affair, Jackson made promises to Wendy: how he would leave his wife, how he and Wendy would be together, how he would work it out. He did not have a single clue how he might fulfil his promises, even as he made them and even as he believed them. Anyway, Wendy never remotely believed him, even as he made love to her and they lay entwined in each other's arms. And even as he made them.

With Delta, he did the most destructive and revealing thing possible: he over-compensated. He became more attentive, more supportive, more loving, more generous with his time and love.

At first, Delta accepted all this without questioning its cause. They were the golden couple, it was how a golden couple should behave.

But eventually Delta began to question. She was not without

intelligence, she was much sharper, more observant than people thought. She knew something was not quite right, and she was certain she knew what it might be.

She swallowed her pride and one morning, when Jackson was in Phoenix on business, she telephoned Octagon Enterprises and asked to speak to Wendy. It came as no surprise to Delta when the receptionist informed her Miss Brewer was out of town on business, she did not know where.

Shortly after her telephone call, Delta checked through the directory, scribbled a name and address on a piece of paper, backed her Range Rover from the garage and drove into Denver. She hired a private investigator.

While she awaited the outcome of his investigation, Delta maintained the illusion of a perfect, golden couple partnership. She hid her heartache and growing anger from their friends and from Jackson himself. She held his hand and smiled whenever a photographer appeared … and she waited. Time was on her side.

Now Wendy Brewer and Jackson Wellman both had a problem.

FOUR

RACHEL left the office early, after giving up her lunch-time to work through the pile of PR releases requiring translating into decent English for makeweight fillers and several telephone calls to get additional quotes for pieces she needed for her columns.

She beat the early evening traffic build-up through the city centre and stopped to pick up food and wine at her favourite deli.

She parked the Citroen in front of her apartment block on the Malone Road and carried the bags inside.

Kelly, her golden-eyed, ginger Manx cat was stretched out asleep on the sofa, paws twitching as he chased after the birds he never ever managed to catch, not even in his dreams.

She balanced the bags in one arm and bent down to ruffle his ears. He yawned and prised open one eye-lid to look at her.

"Oh how lovely to see you home. Now go away!" she said, "Boy, I think you're developing an attitude problem."

She took the bags to the small kitchen and lined the bottles of wine along a shelf.

The one-bedroom apartment, a gift from Daddy, who ran his own light engineering business in Lisburn and who had married the lovely, if somewhat infuriating, Karen, his Personal Assistant, was in a fashionable part of Belfast. Just down the road was the Queen's University and Botanic Garden, where most mornings Rachel jogged.

The apartment had a small hallway, a lounge, a small bathroom-shower, a small dining area off the small kitchen ... it was, you understand, a small apartment.

Karen, however, had insisted on it being furnished with only the best since Karen did not do the worst. Karen had 'helped select' the furniture – ie: largely paid for it – on, as Rachel realised, the assumption that the gesture would store up valuable Brownie Points.

Actually, Rachel was very fond of her step-mother. Yes, she could be infuriating, but she was certainly one of life's most unforgettable characters. Besides, being a young newspaper reporter was not placed highly on the Best Financially Rewarded Jobs list.

Rachel was an only child. She freely admitted that she was Daddy's Girl. Her mother had died when she was a little girl and Rachel had been raised by her father.

The apartment was bright, cheerful and comfortable. The rose red and cream walls were hung with eye-catching modern prints and, since she had recently started to search them out and collect them, old black-and-white photographs of Belfast.

She checked the time and decided to call her friends Jayne and Sandi to confirm the time of their arrival for dinner and another of their regular gossips. Jayne said she had arranged it for 7.30pm, Sandi said she thought it was 8pm, so they compromised: they would come for 7.45.

She enticed Kelly from his snooze with a tin of his favourite MoggieDins, or whatever it was called, and while he got his nose into the chicken-and-green-peas-in-jelly, or whatever it was, she took a shower.

The girls survived another evening of Rachel's cooking. It was not that she was an absolutely awful cook, just that she would not have commanded her own Kitchen Godess television series. She made the one meal she knew she could manage without having to call an ambulance with a stomach pump: cod in seasoned oatmeal, coated with cinnamon and paprika butter, creamed potatoes, peas and sweetcorn. It was the only meal the girls could recall her ever making them.

The consolation was that it came with several bottles of good wine and hours of lively gossip.

It came, too, with two beautiful silver necklaces for Rachel and Jayne from Sandi's most recent collection.

Though Sandi was not greatly amused when her friends outlined their coming Stateside trip. She was, she threw in, going to Donegal for a couple of weeks to seek inspiration.

Donegal was beautiful, but it somehow failed to measure up to a trans-American journey that took in Boston, Chicago, Denver, San Fransisco, Los Angeles, San Diego …

"And New York!"

Part of Rachel's time-off deal with her Editor was that she should spend several days in New York – "A terrible job, but somebody has to do it!" – and then pick up the coast-to-coast Amtrak trip with Jayne, whose starting point was to be Boston.

Rachel had been put in touch with the New York Police Department's Public Affairs people by the Police Service of Northern Ireland Press people – via Detective Inspector John McMurtry, with whom she and Brian had been closely involved during the serial killing case and what the policeman had dubbed the Karpathos Kaper – and had been promised a member of New York's Finest who had been born in Northern Ireland. He or she would make a terrific feature for the News Letter.

Besides, Jayne would be heavily involved in meetings towards the setting up of her proposed Amtrak documentary and she and Rachel had agreed that work, damn it, came first. Boston would be spared the devastation of their combined life force. The rest of the United States would not, they vowed, be quite so lucky.

Thus, Jayne would fly on Aer Lingus from Dublin to Boston on Monday, June 25 and Rachel to New York on the same day. They would spend several days in their respective cities and would take the Lake Shore Limited on Friday, June 29 to meet up when the two legs of the service came together at Albany.

Jayne would look after all the Amtrak bookings on the Lake Shore Limited, the California Zephyr from Chicago through Denver to San Fransisco and the Coast Starlight from San Fransisco to Los Angeles. She had found the excellent www.amtrak website and had worked out times, routes and sleepers where necessary.

Karen had promised to come up with funding to cover the Amtrak journeys – details to be worked out later- and, since she seemed to know all the right people in the right cities, a "really neat" hotel in Manhattan – the Regency on Park Avenue at South Central Park - which she and Daddy had used many times (he to hide in with a stiff, sustaining G&T while she looted the shops).

It all, Sandi had to agree, sounded quite exciting. Not Donegal, certainly, but exciting.

FIVE

THE three sober-suited and unsmiling businessmen looked out of place. They sat at a table at the back of the busy, compact Italian restaurant on Manhattan's 86th Street, just around the corner from Lexington Avenue where the Upper East Side meets Yorkville. Around them sat noisy family groups and young lovers.

The three businessmen were not lovers; at least, not of the Moon in June, Hearts and Flowers variety. They got misty-eyed over balance sheets and cash flows and bank accounts hidden in small, obscure banana republics and Caribbean islands. In Switzerland, the Channel Islands, maybe. Where no suspicious tax department would think of looking. Or, if it did, would not get near to checking out the accounts.

They also got misty-eyed – cold, dark, misty-eyed – when they thought of what should have been hidden away but was not. Such thoughts occupied their minds as they sat in The Puglia Garden Restaurant, absently toying with their food.

They were men who did not get angry, they got even. They lived in the shadows, on the fringes, behind the scenes. They worked on behalf of other shadowy men who could provide vast amounts of money for vast amounts of enterprises ... no questions asked. They were wealthy beyond the conventional understanding of wealth, they funded small countries and large global corporations with never a second thought. And if their terms were not met, if a 'client' was foolish enough to cross them ... well, that was when they got even.

They sat at their table and discussed the little local difficulty they had encountered in Northern Ireland. They had provided funding for an ambitious project on the outskirts of Belfast and their terms had not been met.

Their 'client' had thought them foolish and had crossed them by laundering away much of their money in various off-shore and secret accounts. Their 'client' had paid the ultimate price for his foolishness, an associate had been arrested by the police, another associate had also been disposed of.

But they had still to track down their missing, hidden millions. Some of the money had been recovered but in their terms it hardly counted as anything more than week-end pocket-money, a meal here and a bottle of fine wine there. They required recovery of all of what had been stolen, their associates demanded it, as did their personal reputations.

They sat at their table, the three sober-suited businessmen, and discussed quietly what needed to be done.

The first, most important, thing was that they needed to know where the missing money was and how they could retrieve it. The jailed associate would be reached and "persuaded" to reveal the whereabouts of the various accounts and the account numbers. The "persuasion" would, they had been assured by their Northern Ireland contacts, be thorough and would leave a lasting impression. No effort would be spared to obtain the necessary information.

The second, only slightly less important, hardly worth calculating, thing was to see how much was known about the missing money by several fringe players in the drama, people who knew people who knew about the money and who might, in turn, know where it was and how it could be retrieved.

They spoke, leaning close together across the table, of logistics, of dispatching an operative, of fees and expenses, of "wrapping the matter up", of "completion" and when they had finished their discussion the taller of the three walked from the restaurant to a waiting limo, climbed into the spacious back and as it weaved through the evening traffic down Lexington towards Midtown he made a telephone call.

Events were set in motion.

Marvin Garstein listened silently to his caller, punctuating the one-sided conversation with nods and the scribbling of several short notes on the pad he kept at the side of his telephone. When his caller had concluded, Marvin muttered a brief "Yeah" and replaced the receiver.

He paced his Murray Hill loft-apartment and worked out a timetable. The apartment was large and sparsely-furnished – minimalistic, he preferred to call it – and occupied most of the top – fourth

– floor of what had been a 1950 red-brick warehouse-factory.

He sat at his desk, opened his laptop computer and tapped into the British Airways web. He scrolled through the list of flight times for the following day and when he had decided on one that suited him he ordered a first class single ticket in the name of Martin Demme, giving his American Express card number for that name. He checked the details and, satisfied, he sent the order. Presently it was confirmed and he printed out the confirmation.

He went to a small wall safe hidden behind a framed Metropolitan Museum of Art print of a John Leslie Breck river scene – he loved its calm realism – and removed a steel box. He turned the dial and opened the lid, and counted out $5,000 which he folded into a wallet alongside the flight document.

He walked across the bare wooden floor with its expensive, brightly-patterned, scattered Mexican rugs to his bedroom and slid open a wall-length mirrored walk-in wardrobe. He selected several plain white shirts, a collection of striped ties, black socks, plain white T-shirts and underwear. He flicked along the rail of suits and chose a dark blue Armani. He added a black English-tailored blazer and a pair of grey trousers.

From the rack along the floor of the wardrobe he lifted a pair of black Italian shoes. He packed everything into a black leather week-end shoulder-bag. Whatever else he needed he could always purchase in Belfast; he believed in travelling light.

He thought about the sort of weather he might encounter in Belfast in April-May – bloody Brit weather, the sun shines in January and it pisses with rain in summer – and opted for a tan Burberry trench-coat.

From a locked drawer behind the suits he took out a United States passport in his own name and a United Kingdom one in the name of Martin Demme: always easier to get through the Heathrow checks with a local passport and to return through Kennedy with a Stateside one.

The details were always important. Marvin was a man for details. Marvin was good – hold that thought: he was the best – at what he did.

He checked his Rolex and figured out the time difference. It would be around midnight in Belfast. So what, he shrugged, his contacts in Belfast were getting paid enough to stomach the inconvenience of a late call.

He made the call, brushed aside the complaints and told his contact when he would be arriving and to have the necessary equipment ready for delivery when and where he instructed upon his arrival. While the voice at the other end of the line was still bitching, he replaced the receiver. Call themselves an army, bunch of crapping amateurs.

He gave it a couple of hours and returned to his computer, opening it on his on-line banking account: the money, all $25,000 of it, his fee, had been deposited. He shut down the computer, locked it in the desk and poured himself a fresh orange juice.

Business was good these interesting days.

He awoke early the following morning. While he waited for the fresh coffee to perc he re-checked his documents and put them back in the bag. He grabbed a quick shower and shave and brought a toilet-bag from the bathroom and put it into the bag, placing it just inside the door to his apartment.

He poured himself a mug of black coffee and towelled himself dry. As he drank the coffee he ordered a limo to pick him up at 12.30pm for a run to Kennedy.

He planned to fly to London, spend a couple of days there and take the shuttle across the Irish Sea to Belfast. He liked London, some relaxing R&R would set him up.

He sat in his favourite brown, cracked-leather Gentleman's Club chair and opened an A-4 manilla envelope. He slid its contents onto his knees and picked up a newspaper cutting in a clear, plastic folder. He ignored the story, instead concentrating on the photo-by-line: EXCLUSIVE: By Rachel Andrews.

He checked in at the British Airways desk two-and-a-half-hours before his flight – he never liked to be rushed – and settled in a corner of the Executive Lounge with a cup of coffee.

He had a copy of the day's New York Times draped across his knee but his thoughts were on the tasks ahead and how to complete them successfully.

The brief he had been given was a simple enough one: a case of either this, or that.

The this part required him to uncover the details of where the money had been hidden away: what off-shore banks, what the account and/or code numbers were, how best to return it to the people who had donated it in the first place.

This, he realised, would not be an easy task. The money could be anywhere, and nobody was certain now how much of it had actually been stolen. A conservative estimate was in the region of two, possibly three, million.

One person, for sure, knew where the money was … and that person was currently in the hands of the Northern Ireland police. And Meredith Harling, whose husband, Max, had salted it away, before his 'untimely' death, was not about to reveal its whereabouts.

Max – the late Max – had perpetrated a clever con on his American backers. He had taken over a small religious group in Belfast and turned it into a vast and profitable empire … and then he had become greedy. He had formulated an elaborate plan to build a Tabernacle on the outskirts of Belfast, with seating for several thousand, with audio and visual studios, a radio and television station, a printing press for magazines and books. He had enlisted financial backing from America … and he had deposited it around the world, in obscure banking establishments under various names and with virtually unbreakable codes and account numbers.

Now, only Meredith – who had added even more confusion to any potential search by re-depositing the money in her own obscure banking establishments under her own ficticious names and equally unbreakable codes and account numbers – knew where the treasure was hidden.

Marvin faced the difficult task of getting to Meredith and extracting this information from her.

The that part was a much more simple task: if he could not obtain the information then he was, bluntly, to ensure that Meredith pay, and pay dearly, for what she had done. It mattered not in what cell she was incarcerated, he and his associates in Belfast would reach her.

There was, though, another avenue that required exploration. Rachel Andrews had been the girlfriend of Coren Armstrong, and he had been one of Max and Meredith's closest associates; indeed, he had been Meredith's lover.

There was the possibility – at least in Marvin's estimation – that Coren had told the newspaper reporter where the money now was. It was a long shot, but Marvin had to take that shot, had to leave no stone unturned, had to satisfy himself that Rachel either did or did not know.

And whether she did or did not know, she, too, needed to be disposed of.

It was either this or that. Black or white. No in-between. No loose ends. This or that.

He sat in the British Airways lounge and worked out his plans. He glanced around at his fellow passengers; two business types working on laptops and scribbling notes on yellow legal pads while clutching mobile 'phones to their ears; across the room a striking, dark-haired woman idly flicking through a copy of Vogue, her long, shapely legs crossed carefully to reveal a promising hint of thigh; a smiling, blonde receptionist fussing at her computer to ensure her charges were eventually dispatched on the correct flights; a man at the hospitality cabinet opening a small bottle of whiskey and pouring it into a glass.

Only the striking, dark-haired woman with the legs interested him. He had some five hours to see what might come of that interest. Always assuming, of course, that she was going to London and not some other destination served by British Airways.

The receptionist checked her computer and fingered the tickets on her desk. She lifted two – for the next flight: to London – and walked across the lounge. She stopped at the striking, dark-haired woman, smiled and handed her a boarding pass.

The woman uncrossed her legs and began to gather her magazines and a light, tan briefcase.

Marvin watched this activity as the receptionist moved towards him for the same ceremony of the smile, the presentation of the boarding pass and the announcement that she would escort him and the lady down to the aircraft in five minutes.

In silence, the three made their way from the lounge – no need to force the conversation, he had some five hours – and along the corridor to the 'plane, where the blonde receptionist delivered them into the hands of another blonde, the stewardess.

She glanced at their boarding passes and led them left into the First Class section.

He watched as the dark-haired woman removed her black suit-jacket. She wore an expensive cream blouse, more like a man's shirt, and had a gold pendant swinging on a thin gold chain around her neck, the pendant glinting in the swell of her breasts.

The stewardess took the jacket and his own jacket and hung them at the entrance to the section. He watched as the dark-haired woman reached to the luggage-bin above her head and placed her briefcase into it, closing the lid down. She was braless, he noticed, for the cool of the First Class had suddenly stiffened her small nipples.

She turned and sat down, smiling absently at him. He nodded a silent greeting and took his own seat, reaching for the inflight magazine. Casual, five hours to go.

They were initially the only First Class passengers but just as the other passengers had been directed to their seats at the back of the 'plane a small, fat, perspiring man in a too-heavy pin-striped suit ran down the corridor and panted into the section. He settled in a seat three rows up in the front row and promptly fell asleep.

Marvin opted for the strategy of casual indifference. During the flight he walked twice to the washroom to splash cold water on his face. He returned to his seat, one row in front of her, dabbing at the droplets. He acknowledged her with just a brief nod and a smile. She glanced up and smiled back.

As they walked through Heathrow after collecting their luggage, he kept several paces behind her. He carried the shoulder-bag and his laptop. She pushed a cart with two large leather cases balanced on it.

He watched to see where she was going: to a waiting car, perhaps; to a taxi, perhaps; to the Heathrow Express surface train to Paddington, perhaps; to the Piccadilly Underground Line, perhaps. She was going towards the Heathrow tube station. He followed.

He stood along the platform from her and as the train hummed into the station he made his move. She lifted one of the cases from the cart and slid it across the floor of the train to the luggage space at the opposite door. He walked forward, lifted the other case and carried it on, sliding it alongside its companion.

She was certainly a looker, in the cool-distant manner of a glass ceiling-smashing female executive. Even after the flight and the recycled, drying air of the cabin her dark hair still glistened. She looked as good at the end of her journey as she had sitting in the Kennedy lounge.

He had caught a glimpse of the tags on her cases: Elizabeth Houston c/o The Howard, 12 Temple Place, West End, WC2R 2PR: Room 151. So, he already knew her name and where she was staying. And where he would be staying also.

He followed her into the train, setting his own bag alongside hers, and sat beside her.

"I'm Martin Demme," he said.

"Well," she said, in an English accent, "we meet, eventually. I'm Elizabeth Houston. Are you on business?"

"Yes, for just a few days," he said, "Then I'm going over to Ireland for a couple of days. I'm in the publishing business. Nothing too exciting, just technical manuals for the oil industry. I'd guess you're, let's see now ..."

"Self-employed," she offered, "I run my own company: PR and marketing for the fashion industry."

"How interesting. Here, in London?"

"Well, we do a lot of work in London, of course, but we're actually based in the West Country, in Hereford ... do you know it?"

"I've certainly heard of it. It's a beautiful part of the world, I hear: old cathedral city, famous for cider and those big, red-and-white bulls. Isn't it a bit far out from the glittering world of fashion, though?"

"Sometimes not far enough. I do a lot of travelling – New York, Paris, Milan, the fashion spots – so I figured it didn't matter all that much where I had the office. I can get into London quite easily, quite quickly. I have a small office near the Embankment, just two rooms and a receptionist with the best polished nails in the city ..."

He laughed.

"Yes, I know what you mean. You just can't get the staff these days."

"I don't mind. All she has to do is look pretty and answer the 'phone. The rest of us – I have five people working for me – just get on with it."

He thought he had better beat her to the next piece of information.

"I'm staying at The Howard," he said.

"Well, that's a coincidence ... so am I. It's near the office. I have to meet some clients this evening in the hotel's JAAN restaurant and then tomorrow I'm going back to Hereford."

"Perhaps we could meet for a coffee or a drink after we check in?"

She looked at him, liked what she saw.

"Yes, I think that sounds very civilised."

At the reception he played the gentleman and stood back while the girl behind the desk confirmed her pre-booked room. Elizabeth and the girl, clearly not strangers, chatted for a few moments and as Elizabeth turned and followed the porter wheeling her cases towards the lift she said: "Shall we say in 45 minutes, I need a shower. We can meet in the bar."

He nodded and watched her walk away: long legs, neat ass, confident stride. Good work.

He stepped to the desk and asked for a room, which luckily they had. In his room overlooking the River Thames, he stripped off and shaved and took a shower: hot, scalding followed by cold, freezing. Refreshing. He opened his bag and took out fresh boxers, a fresh pair of socks, a fresh white shirt and a dark blue tie with thin red stripes.

He was waiting for her in the bar when she arrived. Her hair was still sleek and damp, the short strands combed neatly behind her ears. She wore a knee-length black dress with an enticing V cutting between her breasts. A small, yellow stone dangled on a silver chain. She wore just a touch of make-up, allowing her natural skin-tones to glow against the pale-red lipstick. She had a small, black, beaded evening-bag slung over her right shoulder.

He rose from his stool as she came alongside him.

"Name your poison," he said.

"A gin and tonic, I think."

He turned to the barman and held up his right forefinger and pointed to his own glass. Its clear contents bubbled around two ice-cubes, but since he did not drink spirits it was merely a plain tonic.

He raised his glass and clinked it against hers. He pointed across the lounge to a table at the window overlooking the river and walked her towards it, his hand pressed gently into her back.

"It's a lovely hotel, I can see why you like it," he said.

"It's become a home from home. And it's even better when I can spread the cost around my clients. Appearances are everything in the PR world."

The conversation flowed freely between them. He was making progress, excellent progress.

An hour later she checked her watch and, with genuine reluctance, said she needed to grab a nap before her meeting, and to go through her notes. She stood up. He joined her.

"What excitement have you lined up for this evening?" she asked.

"No dull client meeting, but I think a nap also. I guess I'll just work on some editing – really exciting stuff, like an article about the sharpest drill bits to use on hard rock. Two sentences of that and I'll be fast asleep.

"Say, if you have time before you head West tomorrow - Hereford is West of here, isn't it? – maybe I can buy you lunch in some Ye Olde London pub: a sandwich and a pint of warm beer, very traditional."

She nodded: "And that sounds very civilised as well. Don't work too hard."

He sat down and finished his drink, then returned to his room. It was just after 3pm. He stripped to his boxers, pulled the drapes closed and stretched out on the top of the big, soft bed. He slept for over an hour.

He showered and changed into another fresh shirt. He took the lift – elevator: bloody Brits just don't speak the same language – to the lobby and changed an American Express travellers' cheque into £50: bloody awful exchange rate. The man slid five £10s across the marble desk-top and he nodded a thanks, folded the notes into his shirt pocket and walked out.

He found a Marks and Spencer store and bought several plain white shirts. He always travelled light, always bought what he needed as he went along. Used his purchases for a day or two and disposed of them. The less unnecessary baggage the better. One day, he reckoned, he'd get it down to the very barest of essentials: what he wore and a toothbrush in an inside pocket. He could even dispose of the toothbrush … what he wore. And, of course, his laptop.

He bought a copy of the Evening Standard, found a pub along the riverfront on his way back to The Howard, ordered a Coors and took it back outside to a wooden bench. He sipped the beer straight from the bottle and flicked through the newspaper: OK, so Blackburn Rovers had beaten Tottenham Hotspur 2-1 … but how had the Mets done?

He rolled the newspaper and tucked it under his arm, picked up the M&S bag and walked back to the hotel.

He made several telephone calls to Belfast – his contacts were working on getting close to Meredith Harling and what he had requested to be delivered to his city centre hotel in two days time – and ordered a light meal from Room Service.

He finished the meal and placed the tray outside his door.

He watched CNN on the television … and waited.

At first he didn't hear the gentle tap-tap-tap on his room door. When he did he smiled and swung his legs from the bed. He peered through the spy-hole, smiled and opened the door.

Elizabeth walked silently past him. She threw a red shawl over the back of a chair and turned to face him. She was wearing a pale blue dress and fashionably high shoes. She kicked them off and sat down on the edge of the bed, her legs crossed and the dress riding up her thigh.

He looked at his watch, it was 10.40pm: "Mission accomplished, I take it?"

"Yes, I got what I wanted: a fat contract to promote their new line of underwear. Not the most stimulating of clients ... so I thought I'd need some stimulating."

"Stimulation is good for the soul," he said, "So, a new line of underwear ... did they give you any free samples?"

"Pointless," she said, "I never wear any."

"You may have to prove that to me."

She stood up and lifted the dress ... case proven.

She was good, too: energetic and inventive, pacing her every sensuous movement to the nth degree. Just the right pressure here, just the right sway of her hips there. She was bloody good.

They made love – no, they had sex – throughout the night and she lay in his embrace, all passion spent, as the first yellow-grey glow of the morning crept sleepily into the sky.

"I must go now," she whispered, "I have a meeting at 9:30."

She threw back the duvet and swung her long legs to the carpet, twiddling her toes in the thick blue pile. She got up from the bed, turned and kissed him on the lips. He reached up and cupped a breast, gently easing her down to him. He slowly licked the nipple. She moaned but drew from him and pulled the dress over her naked body.

At the door she looked back: "I'll be free at 12.30pm at the latest. Are you still on for that lunch?"

He smiled: "You bet. I'll meet you in the lobby at 12.15."

She blew him a kiss, peered out into the corridor and departed.

He got out of the bed – boy, she was good! – grabbed a cold shower, dressed in a fresh shirt, black jeans and tan deck shoes. He checked the room to make sure nothing would be left behind, threw what he needed into his bag, collected his laptop and walked down the stairs. He paid his bill with cash, assured the receptionist he had enjoyed his stay and left.

He walked to the nearest underground station serving Victoria and there bought a ticket for Gatwick. He caught the late morning flight to the George Best Belfast City Airport.

The airport had, he had read once, been named after some soccer player … yeah, like he gave a rat's ass. In the States soccer was played by teenage girls and watched by yummy mommies with nothing better to do with their time. It hardly counted as a sport at all.

He toyed with the in-flight magazine and sipped at a plastic carton of bitter-tasting black coffee. The 'plane was full and he was crammed against the window, a fat, sweating business type beside him in the middle seat and a young, nondescript girl in the aisle seat. Not exactly a transport of delight.

The 'plane dipped to port and shredded down through the clouds, swooping across Strangford Lough and across the Ards Peninsular to Belfast Lough. He leaned forward and looked down at the tiny islands dotting Strangford, at the large homes that occupied some of the islands.

Across the Peninsular the 'plane turned to the left and he felt the jolt as the under-carriage whirred into place. The 'plane passed the neat little town of Holywood on the left and made a smooth, one-bounce landing.

It circled around on the runway and trundled slowly to the terminal. Good flight, he thought, smooth and on time. The usual request for the passengers to remain seated until the 'plane had come to a complete standstill was, as usual, totally ignored. Almost as one the passengers unclipped their seat-belts, jostled in the aisle and began pulling out their luggage from the overhead bins. Why? They weren't going to get off any quicker, he thought.

Nor did they. The stewardess requested everyone to please remain seated, as instructed, as the steps had not been brought to the 'plane. She almost ended the speech with a resigned sigh since she knew nobody would take a blind bit of notice. Nor did they.

He folded his newspaper and pushed it into the string holder in front of him.

So how come, he wondered, the steps were not in place? Was their arrival a sudden, unexpected surprise? Did a couple of guys in the control tower glance up in stunned awe and say: "Bugger me, there's a bloody 'plane coming in to land!"

Did the people in London forget to tell the people in Belfast that a 'plane had taken off and would, all things being equal, be arriving in their neck of the wood in, say, one hour's time?

The steps were eventually found and brought to the 'plane. The passengers, who had remained standing throughout, filed bovine-like through the door.

He collected his bag from the carousel and walked out of the airport to the waiting taxis.

From London he had checked ahead and found a new, luxury hotel smack in the middle of the city … yeah, like that was a distinct advantage being stuck in the middle of Belfast. But, the luxury part appealed to him. Hay, his associates back in NYC wanted a job done, they paid for it … every which way.

He fished a piece of paper from his jacket pocket to remind himself where he was going and leaned towards the passenger-side window: "Merchant Hotel."

The taxi turned from the airport, joined the flow of traffic through East Belfast, past the big yellow cranes – Samson and Goliath - to the right at what had once been the world's largest shipyard at Harland and Wolff and over the Lagan.

The hotel was, he conceded, pretty spectacular in an in-your-face sort of way. It had once been a bank and, he discovered when the receptionist checked him in, the suites were named after famous local writers. His was the C.S. Lewis, whoever he was.

He undressed, took a shower and sat on the bed to reach for the 'phone. After several rings the 'phone was answered.

"What!"

"This must be the Welcome to Belfast committee," he said.

"Oh, it's you …"

"It would appear so," he said, "But enough of this jolly chatter … where are we?"

"Where are we?"

"Yes," he said, "as in what is the current situation …"

"The current …"

"Oh, for fuck sake you Irish moron … have you any news about Harling?"

"Oh, yeah. We got word to us that she's being brought to Belfast on Thursday for some medical thing. We can arrange for a detour, like, you know … grab her and, like, take her to a safe house …"

"Very droll," he said, "Take her to a safe house, I like that. Take her to a safe house and beat the crap out of her until she tells us where the fucking money is. You Irish really do have a gift for words. So, do it ... keep me informed where this safe house is."

"Yeah, like ..."

He put the 'phone down. Today was Tuesday, two days of kicking his heels in Beautiful Downtown Belfast. OK, all part of the job. At least, he had Thursday to look forward to."

SIX

RACHEL walked from the City Hall, closing the notebook as she went. She had been at the launch of an up-coming festival to celebrate the fact that Northern Ireland was no longer the War Zone – it was, Sandi had wryly commented, now being terrorised by peace – and everybody was madly in love with everybody else. The festival was called Diversity Moving On, which said a great deal and absolutely nothing at all but managed not to offend anybody. The name was even printed on the glossy programme in English, Irish and Ulster-Scots.

Welcome to the New Belfast.

She looked to her right, across the neat, statue-filled lawn in front of the impressive Portland stone building, and checked the time on a building at the corner of Wellington Place and Donegall Square West, where the buses were lined up. She had arranged to meet with Karen, her step-mother, in one of the city's growth-industry cafes, though she now couldn't remember which one.

She sat on a bench and took out her mobile, dialling Karen's number.

"Darling, it's you," Karen trilled.

"Yes, I had a quick look and there I was. I've forgotten where exactly we're supposed to be meeting."

"Silly, in town …"

"Yes, I know that. But where, exactly, in town? The name of the café, the street, the number … exactly."

Silence. There seemed to be some sort of information overload malfunction at Karen's end: one question would have been sufficient for Karen to grapple with.

Rachel took it back to Square One: "Look, why don't we meet at Café Orient, that's in Lombard Street? You can park in the Castle-

45

Court and walk across. I'm at the City Hall right now so I'll go grab a table and meet you there. OK?"

She thought she could hear small wheels grinding in Karen's head, then: "Yes, that's lovely: Café …"

"Orient …"

"Yes, that's lovely: what street did you say?"

"Lombard, out the front door of CastleCourt, turn right, cross the road, walk towards Rosemary Street Church, the café is opposite it … opposite a sex shop."

"A what?"

"Sex shop … S-E-X, as in plastic nurses uniforms, lace panties, peek-a-book bras, crotch …"

"Yes, dear, I get the picture. I'll meet you there …"

"Not in the sex shop, unless you really want to, in Café Orient."

Rachel smiled as Karen rang off.

She waited in the restaurant, got through two mugs of coffee and an egg salad roll and eventually Karen arrived, laden with two Selfridge's bags.

"You shouldn't have rushed," Rachel said.

"Just nipped in to see what they had," Karen said, "Couldn't resist."

"I knew I'd made a mistake telling you to park within a dozen miles of CastleCourt. Wasn't there anything you fancied in the sex shop? I think dad might have fancied the schoolgirl look."

Karen waved away the very thought and reached for the menu. She did her Queen-saluting-the-adoring-throng flick of her hand and ushered a waitress to the table to take her order.

"So what little stories have you been writing today?"

Karen knew that her step-daughter was a reporter but somehow laboured under the confusion that she still did not know what she actually did for a living.

"I was at the City Hall for the launch of a new festival. I'll go back to the office and write it up this afternoon."

"That's nice, darling. Will it be in the 'paper tomorrow?"

"Yes, it's sort of implied. I go to events, I make notes, I go back to the office, I type up the notes, they appear in the next day's 'paper. It's a mysterious process but it seems to work."

"That's nice, darling."

Rachel adored her step-mother but more often than not she felt they lived in worlds that ran alongside one another but never actually touched. Karen, she had long ago discovered, didn't do humour, or irony. But then, Karen didn't do a lot of things that didn't involve lunching with her friends, socialising, spending money and going on frequent vacations with daddy. Karen's one, massive saving grace was that she loved daddy almost as much as shopping.

When Rachel's mother had died her father had raised her himself, juggling his business with creating a perfect childhood. By then Karen had been taken on as his personal assistant, had – as Rachel often remarked to her friends Jayne and Sandi – clearly assisted daddy in all manner of personal ways and eventually married him. By which time Rachel had gone to University and had joined the News Letter and had moved into her own apartment, with some considerable financial assistance from daddy. With, of course, Karen chalking up Brownie Points with additional, and welcome, goodies.

The waitress brought Karen's order and hovered nervously while it passed the taste test. The waitress was dismissed with another twirl of the hand and departed with knitted brows and a mutter.

"So, darling," Karen said, "you and Jayne are still going on your little jaunt? When were you planning to leave?"

Ah, the purpose of the lunch. Time for the sordid monetary details.

"We're looking to the last two weeks in June, first two in July. I'll go to New York and Jayne will go to Boston to start her research into the radio feature she plans to do on the coast-to-coast railway trip. While I'm in New York I'll be gathering some interviews, features, travel pieces, things like that, to send back to the 'paper.

"Then we'll get the train, it's called the Lake Shore Limited and it leaves New York and Boston and the two trains meet up at Albany and go on to Chicago ...."

Rachel stopped, realising that she had probably lost Karen at the "We're looking ..." bit.

"Anyway, long story short, we go across America to San Diego ... er, coast-to-coast."

"That's nice, darling."

Now, thought Rachel, taking a deep and meaningful breath, to the business end of the deal.

"I was wondering if there might be some way of ..."

"Well, darling," Karen said, "you'll obviously need some financial help, won't you? I don't suppose your pay as a reporter will get you further than the nearest bus stop. I'd actually love to come with you, I adore New York ..."

Rachel's blood chilled.

"... but June-July is when daddy and I are thinking of that cruise we've always talked about. Would you mind awfully if I didn't go? You'll be OK on your own?"

"Of course. But about ..."

"But you simply must allow me to pay for the airline tickets and the hotels and your little train trip. I won't hear a word against it."

"That's very generous. I promise I'll pay you back ..."

"Well, we can sort all that out later. I mentioned when you first thought about the trip that I know a perfect hotel in Manhattan, didn't I? Well, just get me dates that you'll be in New York and I'll get in touch with them about a room. I'll talk to daddy and I'm sure he'll come up with a little spending money.

"And we'll look after Willie ..."

"Kelly," Rachel corrected, "His name is Kelly ..."

"Darling, cats don't know what they're called."

"Maybe, maybe not ... but the name he doesn't know he's called is Kelly. Anyway, that would be terrific if you could look after him, he loves it the country."

Kelly did more than love it in the country, he loved the fields around the house in Lisburn, loved chasing the birds and butterflies, even if he hadn't quite grasped the concept that the chase should be followed by a catch. Kelly never caught anything.

Mission accomplished. Rachel celebrated with another mug of coffee. OK, so sometimes the two worlds do manage the odd nudge.

Rachel paid for the lunch and walked Karen up Lombard Street to Royal Avenue where they hugged and air kissed. She watched as Karen crossed the road and turned right towards CastleCourt, where she would doubtless be drawn by a powerful yet unseen force back into one of the shopping centre's many enticing shops like a helpless 'aholic seeking one more fix.

She smiled as Karen was taken to the soothing bosom of the glass and steel building and turned herself towards the City Hall and the new office into which the News Letter had only recently moved from its former soulless HQ in an out-of-the-way avenue of car salesrooms, furniture outlets, carpet stores and equally soulless sundry commercial buildings. The city centre was where the city's oldest newspaper should be … at the heart of things, in the belly of the beast.

Marvin Garstein, as he had decided to call himself today, it being his actual name and he being in need of reminding himself of it, sat on a bench in the City Hall grounds and watched the office girls spread over the lawns. It wasn't that he hated, absolutely hated, Belfast; it had its charms, the office girls for one thing, it was just that he hated having to be away from New York for too long. He could be anonymous in New York; in Belfast he felt he stuck out, the Yank abroad.

Also, whenever he found himself having to be in Belfast there was usually a bloody conclusion to the visit: the little episode with Max Harling sprang to mind. The approaching little episode with Meredith Harling was shaping up into a similar outcome.

But for now he concentrated on the pretty office girls, watching them from behind a copy of The Independent like a newly-graduated spy school student who hadn't quite mastered the stealthy observation technique.

And then he saw her, the little bitch Rachel Andrews. He recognised her instantly, of course, since he had a folder of her photo/by-line stories back in his hotel room. She was another reason for his being in Belfast. If he couldn't get the information his associates had sent him for from Harling he might get them from Andrews. One way or the other he'd discover what, if anything, she knew about the missing millions.

He watched as Rachel left the path and walked across the lawn. He waited until she exited the grounds past the big wheel and the Titanic Memorial, folded his newspaper and walked quickly after her.

He followed her to the News Letter office in the Metro Building on Donegall Square South and from across the street watched as she collected some mail from the receptionist, shared a brief joke and disappeared.

I know where you live, lady; I know where you live. The pieces were falling into place.

Feeling good, things were heading in the right direction, he walked back through the city centre to his hotel. He treated himself to a tonic from the bar before going to his room to make a telephone call.

What he heard made him feel even better. Early on Thursday morning, a source inside Hydebank Wood Women's Prison just south of Belfast had informed his contact, an unmarked car – they even had the registration number – would take Meredith Harling to the Royal Victoria Hospital for further treatment to the injuries she had received in Karpathos. Only the car would not make it to the hospital.

Traffic at the time of the move – around 6.30am – would be light and arrangements would be made for an accident, much confusion and the taking of Harling. When they had her at the safe house he would be collected from the hotel and taken to her ... for their little chat.

Then he would learn where she had salted away the millions she and her husband, Max, had skimmed off from their Tabernacle scam of the previous year. The millions his associates in New York had invested and foolishly lost ... his associates in New York did not like being made to look foolish, let alone losing money.

If she gave him the information he, and his associates, required he might – just might – deposit her back on the streets of Belfast to take her chances ... if she didn't; he merely smiled at the alternatives.

If he did not get what was required from Harling he would turn his attention to the little reporter bitch who had been banging the Harling's associate and who might have picked up the information from their pillow talk. If she failed to come through; he merely smiled at the alternatives.

He knew where she lived.

He returned to the bar for another refreshing tonic, grabbed a meal in the restaurant and slept deeply.

The pick-up had been accomplished with surprising ease. The Ford carrying Meredith Harling, the driver and a male and female nurse turned from the prison gates and headed into the city centre. Traffic was light to non-existent and even the dark Land Rover that eased from the kerbside just along from the gates and fell in behind caused no concern. Not even when it gathered speed and swerved in front to block its passage.

The rest was easier than the three men, now with balaclavas pulled over their faces, thought it would be. The driver kept the engine of the Land Rover ticking over, his two companions jumped out, smashed the Ford's windows, pulled open the rear door, struck the male nurse with a baseball bat and dragged Meredith Harling out.

They carried her to the Land Rover and threw her into the back.

"Not a sound, not a single fucking word," one of the men warned her.

The task had been completed in a matter of minutes, all with not another single vehicle in sight. By the time one did show up they would be long gone. To the safe house.

The mobile on his bedside table tinkled and Marvin roused himself and brought it to his ear.

"We have the package," the voice said, "Go to the corner of Bridge Street and High Street, a green Vauxhall will pick you up in 45 minutes."

SEVEN

PRETENDING was easy; all you had to do was, well, pretend. Pretend that everything was normal, that life was rolling along on its usual, smooth, loving path. Pretend that there was nothing, absolutely nothing, spoiling it.

Delta Dubette-Wellman found it ever so easy to pretend. Pretending was easy. She held hands with Jackson Wellman when they attended the opera and ballet, when they exchanged loving smiles as they chatted with friends at a new exhibition at a new and fashionable gallery, when they hosted a gala evening for the University of Colorado, when they were photographed for the society pages entering or leaving the theatre ... pretending was easy.

She even pretended – quite magnificently – when she found herself in the company of Wendy Brewer, exchanged pretend small-talk when she visited the offices of Octagon Enterprises to meet Jackson for lunch.

But as well as pretending, Delta Dubette-Wellman also worked on perfecting something far more important: a plan.

Jackson and Wendy were the key characters in her plan, the stars of the drama she was formulating in her head: Revenge, a drama starring Jackson Wellman and Wendy Brewer, co-starring Delta Dubette-Wellman, written, produced and directed by Delta Dubette-Wellman from an original idea by Delta Dubette-Wellman.

And on this occasion there would be no pretending.

The summer sun dappled through the trees, the leaves fluttered by a soothing breeze that did not diminish the evening warmth. Delta and Jackson sat in the deep, cushioned wicker seats on the veranda of their Denver home. The granite-stone, Edwardian three-storey, built in the early decade of the 20th Century by a lumber baron in 40 acres of woodland, lay on the Southern edge of the city, near enough to the bustling Denver downtown area and far enough away for quiet relaxation.

She had made a special effort to look at peace, and, not that she ever needed to, a special effort to look beautiful. Delta was beautiful, all of Denver thought so, said so. But today she surpassed even that.

She wore an ankle-length cream linen dress that teased the eye with its hint of brief white panties underneath. Her long hair was tied back in a ponytail and topped by a wide-brimmed straw hat. She rested a copy of Cosmopolitan on her raised knees and held a long-stemmed glass of chilled white wine lifted from a small, round glass-topped table at her side.

Across from her Jackson wore fashionably faded blue jeans, an open white linen shirt and tan deck-shoes. He had an open leather folder of papers on his lap and beside him sat a glass of Black Bush, his favourite Irish whiskey. From time to time he would make a note in the margin of a letter or paper and look up at Delta with a smile.

She smiled back.

Somewhere among the trees they could hear the excited barking of the two Golden Retrievers, Lee and Jubal, but the dogs clearly had more important things to do than complete the perfect picture … they hardly needed to for wasn't this Jackson Wellman and the beautiful Delta Dubette-Jackson, the Golden Couple?

Megan, their Scottish maid, came out onto the veranda from the kitchen and asked if they required anything else. She reminded them that she was going to a meeting in the local church. They did not require anything else and told her to enjoy herself.

"That reminds me, darling," Delta said, "I have to go to Boulder at the week-end, there's a meeting about the dance festival. I nearly forgot about it until Megan reminded me. You don't mind, do you?"

Jackson smiled: "No. I'll miss you, darling, but I can catch up with some work at the office. You go and enjoy yourself."

That night Delta forced herself to enjoy their lovemaking. In truth, she did not need on this occasion to pretend.

When she awoke the following morning Jackson had already left for the office. But he was not aware that Delta knew what he had planned for the week-end. She got out of bed, stretched and took a shower, standing naked in the bedroom to gently towel herself dry. A sultry morning breeze billowed the curtains at the open window and she fluffed her hair to dry in the sun.

She dressed in a light blue shirt and white trousers, rang down to the kitchen to have cook and Megan set up a breakfast of orange juice, coffee and one lightly-toasted buttered muffin on the veranda. The morning was going to be a busy one.

She took a telephone directory, her personal contacts book and cellphone to the linen-draped table with the single yellow rose in a small vase, poured a cup of black coffee and flicked through her contact book.

She thumbed the number of the St Julien Hotel and Spa on Walnut Street in Boulder and ordered a room for the week-end: Friday-Saturday-Sunday. She gave her American Express card number and thanked the girl on the other end.

She opened the Denver telephone directory at the Car Hire section and traced down the various companies to select a suitable one, not one of the majors like Avis. She scribbled the number of her selection on a pad and ordered a small – fast, though she did not mention this fact – car for a Friday pick-up. Again she gave her card number.

She made several personal calls to friends, underlining the proposed trip to Boulder, and over the remains of her coffee made suitable small-talk.

Jackson arrived at the Octagon building at 7.45am when only a handful of employees were in. He chatted with the two security men who sat behind a desk and a bank of flickering TV monitors in the lobby and walked to the elevators. He rode up to the tenth floor, deserted, and along the red carpeted corridor to his office with its view of the city and of the distant Rockie Mountains to the right.

He poured a glass of cold sparkling spring water and swished it around his mouth before removing his jacket and sitting at his desk.

He worked on some papers until the clock on the wall across from his desk clicked to 9am. He called the company pilot and asked that the Lear be made available for a Friday afternoon flight to Glenwood Springs, say around 2.30pm. He called the Hotel Colorado on Pine Street and booked the best double-room for Friday and Saturday, in the name of Wendy Brewer and charged to the Octagon Enterprises account.

At 9.15am he buzzed for Wendy to come to his office.

She knocked gently on his office door and entered. He watched as she walked towards him, athletic, sensual, dressed in a black skirt that was almost but not quite mini, and pink silk shirt. She reached his desk, leaned across it and kissed him on the lips. She smiled and shook a finger at him as he reached for her breast. She sat in a black leather chair and slowly crossed her legs. Eat your heart out, Sharon Stone.

"Is there anything you'd like me to take down, Mr Wellman?"

"Yes. It's not what I'd prefer at this precise moment in time, Ms Brewer, but take down an address: Hotel Colorado, Glenwood Springs, 526 Pine Street, Room 462. And add these dates: Friday, June 15 till Sunday, June 17 …"

She stopped writing, looked at her notes and then at him.

"That's this week-end …"

"Indeed it is," Jackson came around his desk and plucked her from the chair. She lifted her face to his and they kissed, this time she let his hands find her breasts and gently finger her nipples.

"I don't understand," she said.

"Well, let me explain," he said, "Delta has another of her endless committee meetings, in Boulder I believe she said, over the week-end … and thank the Lord for them, I say. So I've conjured up some vital business in Glenwood and, of course, my invaluable personal assistant just has to be there to hold my hand, and anything else she finds of interest.

"I've booked a room – see your notebook – in your name … a week-end in the Rockies, staying at the Little White House of the West. Just you and me, working very hard for the greater good of Octagon Enterprises. What do you say?"

"It's a terrible job, but I say I'll manage to make the most of it."

"I've arranged to take the Lear to Glenwood just after lunch," Jackson had returned to his desk, "I hope you don't mind driving there, best not to push our luck too far by going together. You can take Friday off and make your way there."

"No, that's fine," she said, "It's just over a couple of hours, I'll leave in the morning and check in."

She closed her notebook and leaned again across his desk, kissing him.

Delta finished packing a week-end bag and carried it out to the Land Rover. It was 8.15am and as she opened the door of the vehicle Jackson walked down the steps of the veranda to the pink gravel

56

driveway around the house.

"You have everything, darling?"

She nodded and held out her arms to him. He took her in his arms and kissed her, brushing a hand up the inside of her leg. She moaned softly, she could not stop herself.

"If you keep doing that I might not go to the meeting, darling?" she said.

Jackson slowly withdrew his hand and smiled: "Well, what would the Boulder dance community think if you failed to show up? Go, have a great time, knock 'em dead … I love you."

"Love you, too," she called, blowing him a kiss. She drove around the small lawn in front of the house and down the path to the gates and the road.

She drove into Denver city centre and parked the Land Rover in a multi-storey. She hailed a cab to take her to Zenith Auto Rentals, collected the Ford she had ordered and drove it back to the multi. At the Land Rover she removed her bag and threw it into the back of the rental. She steered the car into the traffic and drove into the city suburbs.

She found a nondescript mall with a passable coffee shop, she bought a magazine and waited.

She had, in her planning, made several assumptions … one or all of them likely, she realised, to go wrong. By establishing a rea-son to be out of town she correctly assumed that Jackson and the little bitch would take full advantage and take off somewhere … anywhere. Or they might not. He had been in such a state of sexual excitement since she had first mentioned Boulder that she figured they would.

What she now had to confirm was where: the Estes Park house? Aspen? New Bloody York? The bitch's apartment? She dismissed Estes Park, too dangerous. New Bloody York, too far. The bitch's apartment, not romantic enough and, again, too dangerous.

Or absolutely nowhere at all. No, she knew they had planned something.

She finished her coffee and strolled around the mall. She grabbed a quick and tasteless lunch in a tasteless restaurant full of obese soccer mums and obese, squabbling children and checked her watch: it was 1.30pm.

She returned to the Ford, sat in the driver's seat and 'phoned Octagon Enterprises. She asked if she could speak to Miss Wendy

Brewer, telling the receptionist when asked that her name was Anderson and she was calling on business from California – God, she hoped the time difference wasn't out of line for such a call. She was put on hold, listening to a reedy-sounding rendition of a violin piece she couldn't place.

"I'm sorry to have kept you waiting, Ms Anderson," the receptionist eventually said, "but Ms Brewer isn't in her office at the moment. I believe she is away on business over the week-end. May I take a message or could you call back on Monday?"

Delta mulled over the information then said: "No, I can call again on Monday," she thought some more and added, "Perhaps I could speak to Mr Wellman ..."

"Yes, just hold and I'll see if he's in ..."

Again with the tuneless violin and again the receptionist: "No luck, I'm afraid, Mr Wellman has gone out of town ... excuse me a moment, what?" there was a muffled conversation between the receptionist and someone else, "I'm told Mr Wellman has taken the company 'plane to Glenwood Springs. He's due back on Monday."

Delta thanked the receptionist and closed her 'cell.

She thumped the dashboard in triumph: "Got you, you cheating bastard!"

She started the Ford and turned it towards Glenwood Springs, some 158 miles to the West, though what precisely she would do when she got there she had not yet worked out ... just something.

Wendy showered, dressed and boiled a kettle for a tea: Earl Gray with a slice of lemon. She blow-dried her hair and flicked through the clothes in her wardrobe. She selected a blue denim shirt and black jeans. Nothing else. She had already packed the clothes she would need for the week-end, everything except nightwear ... she doubted she would need it, even get time to put it on if she had. She sat down and pulled on ornately-decorated – and very expensive – cowboy boots.

It was 10.15am as she walked to the underground car park of her apartment building and put the case into the boot of her Mercedes. She put the hood down and adjusted her sunglasses.

She would take her time getting to Glenwood Springs; she planned to arrive around 1.30. She would find somewhere to have lunch on the way, refresh herself, stretch her legs. She planned to be waiting in the room when Jackson found Room 462.

Jackson relaxed in his deep cream seat as the Lear lifted into a blue sky and sliced through the fingers of clouds. When the 'plane had gained cruising height and levelled out towards Glenwood Springs and the Northern end of the Rockies he poured himself a gin and soda and watched Colorado glide below him.

Delta began to have doubts, the sort of doubts that accompany the thought that it seemed a good idea at the time ... but not so good now. She was driving to Glenwood Springs, but for what? To find out what was going on? Well, she knew already what was going on: her husband was screwing his PA. She had put two and two together and the answer was an emphatic four. She had hired a private detective and he, too, had arrived at four.

But she was driving to Glenwood Springs where they had, she had discovered, arranged a tryst. Glenwood Springs was a big enough place, but not that big. And she was driving to Glenwood Springs to do what, exactly?

She pulled the car – clever of her to have hired a nondescript Ford neither Jackson nor the bitch would immediately recognise – into the dirt siding of the road and got out. The air was bracingly crisp, the trees gently rustling in the June breeze, large birds – vultures, eagles? – soared and swirled above her, somewhere in the distance an elk trumpeted.

She sat on a stump of a tree, kicked off her shoes and stretched her legs. And she began gathering her scattered, random thoughts. What to do, exactly?

She and Jackson had visited Glenwood many times – though she always preferred Estes Park, maybe Vale or Aspen – so she knew she couldn't just swan into the town and ... do whatever.

The thoughts stopped racing and began to form into patterns. Where, for instance, would they stay?

When she and Jackson had visited Glenwood they stayed in the grand old Hotel Colorado, the Little White House of the West, since several Presidents – Theodore Roosevelt and William Howard Taft – had visited. The teddy bear was said to have been invented during the former's visit in 1905.

Jackson wasn't the most original or careful thinker so she guessed that would be his choice, the Hotel Colorado.

So this is what she would do: get to Glenwood, find a hotel or motel off the main strip and see if Jackson and the bitch dared show themselves. They say that if you stop in one place long enough – Trafalgar Square in London, the Spanish Steps in Rome – you'll eventually meet everyone you know in the world. She would find a coffee shop, buy a copy of the Glenwood Springs Post Independent, hide behind it and wait.

God, she thought, she was sitting at the side of the road talking to herself. The people in the few cars that had passed must have wondered about the strange woman sitting muttering to herself like some demented Manhattan bag lady.

Returning to the car she pulled onto the road and switched on the radio, punching the buttons through several all-talk news stations, a couple of C&Ws and a blaring hard rock until she found a classic station.

The dashboard clock flicked to 12.45pm and she estimated that she was 45 minutes from Glenwood Springs.

She looked for signs indicating the turn-off from Interstate 70 along which she was now travelling and eventually they began to appear. She reached Pine Street just as the clock registered 1.30pm.

She stopped opposite the Colorado Hotel entrance and waited. She wasn't sure what she was waiting for but it at least allowed her to catch her breath and make sure the thoughts hadn't taken off again in all directions.

The Italianate hotel, now one of the Grande Dame National Trust's Historic Hotels of America, had been built in the early 1890s by silver magnet and banker Walter Devereaux as a cream-coloured Roman Brick and Peach Blown Sandstone replica of the Villa de Medici. She wondered if papa 'Bull' had ever thought of building a hotel in, say, Estes Park … the Hotel Dubette had a certain something to it.

The Colorado had opened in 1893 with a fireworks display, an orchestra playing in the ballroom for the 300 guest couples. Papa 'Bull' would have been in his glory, all those beautiful women and pretty young wives.

The hotel was even said to be haunted in several rooms. She thought about adding to the number with the ghosts of Jackson and the bitch.

Delta sat in the Ford until the radio station went into a short headline news report. It was 2pm. As she reached to start the car she saw the Mercedes approach the hotel in her rear view mirror. There was no mistaking the driver. So, she thought, the Hotel Colorado it was.

She drove along Grand Avenue and on the outskirts of town she came upon a motel. It looked seedy and in need of paint and repair but the flickering neon sign of The Silver Spur sizzled Rooms Available, TV/Adult, $50 a night. Hardly the Hotel Colorado, hardly what she was used to, but nothing in her life these days was what she was used to.

She slowed to let a lumbering truck and a following line of frustrated cars go past and turned into the largely empty tarmac park in front of the square-shaped compound of rooms. She spotted the office, got her bag and walked to it.

A bell tinkled as she pushed open the door. The office was empty but eventually a man she could see engrossed in a magazine in a back room struggled to his feet and with a heavy sigh came to the desk.

He was unshaven, running to fat and wore a grubby green shirt stained with food down the front. The sleeves were rolled up revealing tattoos of swooping eagles menacing naked women with impossibly large breasts. He had the wet remains of a chewed, unlit cigar chomped between yellow teeth and what he had been reading was, she saw, a porn magazine that he made no effort to hide from her.

"I'd like a room," she said.

"Guess that's why you're here, lady," the man said, sliding a dog-eared book towards her. As she signed in – with a false name – she could feel his eyes on her. She turned the book back to him.

"How long you staying?"

"One night, possibly two."

He glanced at the book: "That'll be $100, pay in advance. You get a refund if you don't stay the two nights."

She paid him cash and he slapped a key on the counter.

"Cabin 14, out, turn left, seven down."

He watched as she left the office: good-looking broad, classy even, certainly not the usual client you get here, good jugs, long legs, great ass ... maybe the old man isn't doing it for her, maybe she's looking for some action. Maybe he'd get lucky tonight.

She found Cabin 14 – a room with a phew, a lumpy-looking double bed with a cigarette-burned cover, a beer-ringed cheap pine table and a decidedly off-white bathroom-shower at the back. She shrugged and threw her bag on the bed.

She went to the bathroom and peeled off her shirt and jeans, just as the man pushed open the door.

"Brought you some soap and towels, no extra charge," he said, taking in the view. The broad wasn't wearing a bra – really good jugs – and only the briefest, most transparent of silk panties.

"Don't you knock!" Delta shouted, "Get out, now!"

The man threw her a leer: "Hay, lady, don't get those lovely knickers in a twist."

He left and she sat down on the bed: "God, what in hell am I doing here?"

Wendy checked in and had her bag carried to her room. It was 2.12. She took a long, refreshing, searing-hot shower, patted herself dry and ordered a bottle of the hotel's best – the very best – champaigne. She put on the pristine fluffy robe to sign for the silver bucket with the sparkling drink tilted in the middle of a nest of ice chunks and two fluted glasses. She took a bottle of Creed Green Irish Tweed perfume from her bag and sprayed behind her ears, on her neck, down between her breasts and between her legs. She relaxed on the bed … ready and waiting.

Jackson told the pilot to come pick him up Sunday afternoon and slipped him a couple of hundred Dollar bills. He walked through the airport and grabbed a cab. When he got to the Colorado he walked with purpose through the crowded lobby and took the elevator to the room, like he had been a guest for weeks.

Delta tried not to think about the state of the bathroom with the dripping shower, the mildewed plastic curtain and the water-stained cubicle tray. She risked a quick shower, washing her hair with the small bottle of cheap shampoo the man had placed on top of the two towels alongside the bar of unwrapped soap. The Hotel Colorado it wasn't.

In a drawer in the bedside table she found a torn Welcome to Beautiful Glenwood Springs brochure and looked through it for a decent café or restaurant … not one where she was likely to run across Jackson and the bitch, just somewhere she wouldn't be poisoned or hit on by some ambitious local stud. The Mountain Grill looked, on paper at any rate, like it wasn't about to be shut down and burned to the ground by a concerned health and public safety inspector. It was on Colorado Avenue, running parallel to Grand and not too far away.

It was actually quite good, all red and blue gingham tablecloths, all worn-plank walls, all candles in wine bottles, though she had to wait for a table at the back since the place was filling up with locals and happy week-enders. Indeed, she was lucky to get a table by herself, albeit one with the washrooms on one side and the kitchen on the other.

A young and pretty waitress – Tracey-Charlene, proclaimed the badge on her uniform – filled a tumbler with ice water and gave her the run-down on what was on the menu, adding with a conspiratorial nod that if it was her she would go for the Choke Chicken and creamed potatoes, vegetables as a side-order and, to follow, New Lime Pie. Throw in a cold Coors and she would not have much to complain about. For good measure, she also threw in a struggling-student-please-tip-generously-have-a-nice-evening smile.

Delta ordered the lot.

"You just visiting?" Tracey-Charlene asked as she organised the knives and forks and napkin.

"Yes, just for a couple of days, on business. Seems a nice place."

"It's not bad," Tracey-Charlene conceded, not bothering the tourist with the thought that as soon as she could collect enough for the fare she'd be outa the place as quickly as a Greyhound could carry her.

"You should visit the hot springs swimming-pool, largest in the world. And the Caverns and Fairy Caves, they're pretty neat. Scenery's neat all around, if you like mountains and rivers."

"I'll give them a go," said Delta, not bothering the waitress with the thought that she would rather visit her husband and the bitch, strangle them and avoid visiting the Glenwood Springs Police Department to answer questions.

She left a generous tip and returned to the motel. She felt the man watching her as she walked from the car to her cabin. Safely inside, she locked the door, slid the chain into place and for good measure pushed the table against the door.

She undressed to her underwear and lay on top of the bed. There was no way she was going to sleep in it, not even throw back the blankets to see what it was like. Surprisingly, she slept soundly until 7.30 the following morning. She dressed and rearranged the furniture before walking to the office to confirm that she would be staying that night.

The man had been replaced by a thin, friendly, middle-aged woman who looked stunned that anyone would want to stay for one, let alone two, nights.

Delta spotted a coffee machine in the corner and fished in her bag for small change.

"Wouldn't waste your money," the women advised, "that thing hasn't worked for years. Even if it did I wouldn't drink the muck."

"Right," Delta said. She could do with a stiff caffeine rush.

"I've just made a fresh pot," the woman said, "Would you like a coffee?"

"Yes, I would. Thank you."

The woman went into the back office and returned with a Homer Simpson mug of black coffee.

She had tasted better but Delta drained the mug and thanked the woman. She drove the car back towards the Hotel Colorado, still unsure of what she was really doing ... stalking, she guessed it would be called.

By 8.30am she was parked opposite the hotel with a clear view of the entrance ahead and to her right. She switched on the radio and listened to a talk show, waiting.

Jackson lay in the big bed and watched Wendy emerge from the bathroom. She was naked and she was beautiful. They had spent the night exhausting themselves with frantic sex.

He knew in his heart the danger of what he was doing, what he was risking ... but he wasn't thinking with his heart. And Wendy was worth all the risk.

"What will we do today?" he asked.

Wendy came to him and reached for him beneath the crumpled sheets, gently fingering him: "We could always find something interesting, don't you think?"

He allowed her to bring him off, lifting his head to kiss her hard nipples.

"Hay, I'm an old guy," he said, "I need to save my energy for later," he slapped her butt, "Go get dressed, we'll have breakfast and go for a drive ... maybe the mountain air will inspire me."

By 9.45 Delta figured they wouldn't be showing. Still screwing, she figured. She started the Ford and drove back along Grand Avenue, searching for a café. She found a car park and walked along Grand, stopping to take a Post Independent from its windowed street stand. She stopped at a café and glanced down the breakfast-all-day menu. She went in.

She took a window table and ordered fresh orange juice, a stack of pancakes with syrup and bacon filling and a black coffee. She took a notebook and pen from her bag to give the impression that she was organising a busy day ahead. She kept a close eye on the street.

And then she made a decision: she no longer cared. As simple as that, it no longer mattered to her how often her husband screwed the little bitch. After all the planning, all the frantic driving, all the furtive sneaking about and watching and stalking … what did it matter?

Only in one respect, she thought as she gazed at the week-end visitors strolling along Grand Avenue, only in terms of getting even, of gaining sweet revenge, of destroying her husband and the bitch. The sheer stupidity of sitting alone in a café on a beautiful Summer morning struck her. What could she have hoped to achieve: burst like a hurricane into the hotel room, create a scene of wild screaming, physically attack them, have every newspaper, magazine, radio and television station from Boston to San Diego hound her?

She was still, always, Delta Dubette – forget the Wellman part, she already had – and a Dubette didn't grab a headline for something as undignified and lurid as that. She would gain her revenge in other ways, ways in which no finger could be pointed in her direction.

She paid for the breakfast and went back to the car. Already a better, more satisfying, far more deadly plan was forming in her mind. Let Jackson and the bitch enjoy their week-end of screwing, she had been foolish to chase after them, she had better ways of getting her own back.

As she hit Highway 70 it was as though Glenwood Springs and what she had done had never happened. She felt light-headed … Jackson and the bitch would know soon enough what she had in mind for them.

The fat lady was still in the wings practising her scales.

EIGHT

HE waited – and waited – and finally the car pulled up at the kerb, the front-seat passenger rolled down the window and waved. He walked to the car and got in. The interior stank of stale cigarette smoke and BO so he rolled down the window, just as the driver lit another one.

He reached over the seat, plucked it from the driver's mouth and stubbed it out on the cracked plastic lining of the door before flicking it onto the street.

The driver tried a menacing glower but it didn't work so he scraped the gears and jerked the car into life. They rode in sullen silence through the busy Belfast streets.

"So where is she?" Marvin asked.

"Safe," the passenger muttered, without turning around, "Safe where we stashed her."

"Is she OK?"

The driver and passenger exchanged a smirk and the driver said: "Oh yeah, she's looking fucking good. Like, she's ready for our little chat …"

"MY little chat," Marvin corrected, "I'll see her alone."

"Maguire won't like that …"

"Like I give a fuck what Maguire likes or doesn't like," Marvin said, "He likes the money we give him, he likes the drugs we get him, he liked the guns we got him … anything else that doesn't sit with him can go screw itself."

The driver shrugged. Like he gave a fuck.

They drove along May Street, past the back of the City Hall on Donegall Square South and along Howard Street. They crossed Great Victoria Street at the Spires Mall – it was also the headquarters of the Presbyterian Church in Ireland, a perfect blending of God and Mammon, it reminded him of Max Harling and his Tabernacle – and drove up the Grosvenor Road.

"OK," Marvin said, "we've done the scenic city tour, when do we reach this so-called safe house?"

"Soon," the passenger said.

Turning right onto the Falls Road they drove into a warren of narrow streets lined by small, red-brick terraced houses, some crumbling towards decay and others, surprisingly, brightly painted and well maintained. Marvin tried to guess what the safe house would look like. He figured it would be on the verge of demolition.

"Just along here, second on the left," the driver said, "We'll park beyond the house and walk down the entry. Don't want to arouse suspicion."

Marvin rolled his eyes and snorted: "Isn't that the idea of the house being safe: nothing about it arouses suspicion … dickhead!"

"We're here," the passenger said, thumbing towards a house.

It was, Marvin noted, suitably nondescript, neither overly-painted nor in a derelict state. Just an ordinary terraced house in an ordinary street. Safe enough, he conceded … well, it wasn't surrounded by gun-toting cops yelling into bull-horns and getting the teargas canisters ready. No thumping helicopters whirring overhead weaving searchlights around the street.

They got out and the driver led them back along the street and into a narrow, paper-blown alleyway behind the houses. They picked their way around gaping black plastic bags, reached a wooden door and he knocked.

"Who is it?" a voice asked.

"Who the fuck do you think it is … the Paisley Memorial LOL Flute Band?" the passenger said, "It's Sean and Dermot, and the Yank. Open the fucking door."

They stepped into a whitewashed yard and crossed to the back door and into a small kitchen. The passenger stopped for a drink of water while the driver took Marvin through to the hallway, pointing up the stairs.

"She's up there, in the back bedroom," he said, "You should wait for Maguire …"

"Like I said before …"

"Yeah, like you give a fuck about Maguire. I'll be sure and tell him your thoughts on that matter."

"Do that very thing, and while you're thinking about it get me a drink."

The driver turned back towards the kitchen.

"A soft ..."

"What?"

"A soft drink, orange or lime, something like that."

The driver shrugged and returned presently holding a bottle of Sprite. Marvin took it and ordered the driver to wait downstairs and keep anybody else away – including Maguire, if he turned up. This was his show from here on in, what he had come to do. He slowly climbed the stairs.

Upstairs he saw, at the top of the landing, a small, blue-and-white tiled bathroom with a large-ish front bedroom to his right. He stepped into it. He was surprised to see that it was clean, with a neatly covered double bed layered with brightly coloured cushions. There was a low dressing-table with a square mirror set against the lace curtained window and a light pine cupboard set in an alcove. He opened the cupboard doors and saw a row of dresses, a man's dark blue suit and several shirts and trousers hanging inside.

He pulled open the drawers of the dressing-table and saw neatly folded blouses, lacy female underwear and socks. On the flower-patterned wall behind the bed there was a framed Discover Ireland tourist print of a mountain and a lake. On the wall beside the bed was a picture of Jesus with a bleeding heart.

So somebody actually lived in the house. He wondered under what circumstances they allowed it to be used for its present purpose: fear, intimidation, belief, hard cash? One thing he surmised: the owners were not currently using the house. Perhaps enjoying an all-expenses vacation somewhere in Spain.

The door to the back bedroom was closed. He heard a faint whimpering from the other side. He turned the handle and stepped inside.

A startled youth, hardly more than 18-year-old, stared wide-eyed at him. The youth was standing beside a single bed looking at Meredith Harling. She lay with her eyes covered, her hands pulled above her head and tied to the iron headboard. She was naked.

"You," Marvin snapped, stepping towards the youth, "Get the fuck away from her, now!"

"But ..." the youth stammered.

"But nothing. Get out ..."

"Maguire ..."

Marvin grabbed the youth by the throat and dragged him to the door. Gurgling and choking, his arms flailing wildly and his legs stumbling, the youth was pushed to the top of the stairs and thrown down them. Marvin listened with pleasure as the body bounced and thumped down into the hallway, listened to the sudden shouting and cursing from below and then he returned to the bedroom.

He untied Meredith's hands and lifted her from the bed, sitting her in the only piece of furniture in the room, a kitchen chair. He retied her hands behind her, tied her legs to the chair legs and sat on the bed looking at her.

She looked a mess. She was still whimpering, slumped in the chair. She was no longer the beautiful, sexy media darling of the newspaper and magazine features, no longer the bright, sassy star of the radio and television panel shows. She had a white, prison-pallor and her once shining, expensively-tended hair hung in damp, dirty strands. The only colour he saw on her face was the browning, yellow bruise below her right eye and the barely healed gash across her cheekbone. Her lips were blue and cracked.

"How different you look, Mrs Harling," he said suddenly. She jerked her head up, turning towards the sound of his voice, "We meet under, shall we say, trying circumstances."

"Who are you?" she said faintly, "Where am I?"

"It really doesn't matter either way," Marvin said, "However, I'm hurt you don't recognise my voice. How soon they forget, eh? To remind you: we met last year when you and Mr Harling – may he rest in deep unease – were lording, no pun intended, it over your adoring flock … and causing my associates a great deal of trouble. Why, I even did you a great personal favour at the time … and, how truly disappointing it is, that you forget. Cast your devious mind back and I'm sure you'll remember who I am."

He waited and eventually she said in a whisper: "Marvin …"

"See, I knew you could never forget me. We have so much in common: the passing of your husband and, of course, the money you have that I and my associates want back.

"So let us not waste any more valuable time … a very simple question requires an equally simple answer: where is the money and how do we get it back?"

"Go fuck yourself," she snapped, straining at the ropes. He smiled, he had to admit she was a tougher cookie than he thought. But a foolish one.

"I don't think I would enjoy that, though under different circumstances you and I might enjoy trying it together. So let me ask you again: where have you hidden the money and how do we retrieve it?"

She spat towards him: "Even if I knew exactly where it was I couldn't tell you ..."

"Oh dear, this is awkward," he rose from the bed and slapped her. She screamed as blood began to trickle from her lips. He grabbed her hair and jerked her upright in the chair, "That was a gentle reminder that I'm here for a serious purpose, as you yourself are: the money, where is the fucking money?"

He waited, watching her fight for composure and breath. He could see what she had once been, desirable, vibrant, sexy. She had even earned a living from what she had been ... once.

He reached to her and cupped a breast. She struggled and twisted to escape. He laughed and released her.

"We could spend a lot of time together, I'd quite enjoy it," he said. He stood at the window looking down into the yard where a man sat reading a newspaper by the back door, "But time is not of the essence. Do you require me to repeat my question?"

The truth was, he realised, that she was not in a position to answer his question. He knew that she and her colleague – what was his name again: Colum, Coren ... that was it, Coren – had salted the money away in various off-shore banks after her husband Max had skimmed it off the funding the New York associates had provided for the proposed Tabernacle outside Belfast. But even if she could recall exactly where the money now was she certainly would not be able to recall the necessary serial numbers, passwords and codes that would make the money available. He guessed he had always considered this possibility.

"If I concede that you are not able to give me the exact details of the various accounts at this moment in time," he began again, "you could do yourself a favour by telling me in what banks and in what countries the money is stashed. I might be in a position to get you out of this mess, accompany you to the banks even."

She merely moaned, and he knew she would not be providing the information he needed. She probably couldn't remember where the money was, almost certainly not whatever codes and account numbers he would require.

He went to the bathroom, opened a small cupboard and found

a plastic tumbler. He cleaned it in the basin with toilet-paper and brought her some water. He held it to her lips as she slurped at it, drops running down her chin.

He wiped some water on her face and sat down with a deep sigh.

"Marvin," she said faintly, "Are you there, Marvin?"

"Yes."

"What's going to happen to me? What are you going to do?"

"Nothing pleasant," he said, "Only you can change the future, you know that. My associates want their money back, you are the only one still alive who knows where it is …"

"I don't," she said, "I mean, I can't remember, I can't remember. I don't remember the banks, I don't remember the account numbers … I don't remember!"

"Then we have a problem, don't we?"

He got up from the bed and stood in front of her. What a mess, a fucking mess, he thought. Meredith was in no position to help him, or herself. He slapped her again and turned from the room, slamming the door shut to block out the sound of her screaming.

Downstairs the driver, passenger and the youth he had thrown from the room sat in the kitchen drinking cans of Guinness.

"Did you get what you wanted?" the driver asked.

"Not yet, but we're getting there," Marvin lied, "Leave her alone and I'll pick it up later."

"The kid will keep an eye on her," the driver said.

"The kid will stay away from her," Marvin said, glaring at the youth, "You'll all stay away from her, got that? Stay away ...," he pointed at the youth, "specially you. If you've been within a mile of her I'll break your fucking skinny neck. You hear me?"

The youth nodded.

"You," Marvin said to the passenger, "get her something to eat, take it to her. Now, do it now!"

He watched as the passenger reluctantly toasted a slice of bread, scrambled a couple of eggs and filled a mug with steaming hot tea. He watched as the food was carried upstairs and into the bedroom.

The passenger returned and as he passed Marvin in the hallway Marvin grabbed him: "That's the last time any of you go into that room, understand?"

"What are you going to do now?" the driver asked.

"I'm going to get out of this rat-hole, get some fresh air. You're going to take me back to the hotel, I have things to do. I'll come back in the afternoon. You have my mobile number, call me around three o'clock and come get me. And nobody go near her."

The driver dropped him off in front of the City Hall and he walked along Donegall Place towards Royal Avenue. He turned right into Castle Place, walked towards the leaning Albert Clock and left into Lombard Street where he found a restaurant at the far corner. He suddenly felt hungry, went in and bought a slice of minced pie, creamed potatoes and a glass of milk. He carried the tray to a booth at the window and mulled over the situation.

When he had finished the meal he walked the short distance to his hotel. At the reception desk he picked up a copy of Belfast In Your Pocket and then he spotted a copy of that day's News Letter.

Splashed above the title was a picture promo ... for Rachel Andrews. He went into the bar, ordered coffee and read:

Coming Soon: ANDREWS IN AMERICA: An Exciting Coast-to-Coast Series from our Star Columnist ... Follow her Exclusive Stateside Odyssey: June and July.

Complications like that he could do without. He went to his room and lay on the bed to consider his next moves.

There was also, he saw, a lengthy report on the search for the missing Meredith: police following up leads, leaving no stone unturned, etc, etc. It had been written by Rachel Andrews and Brian Leonard. He already knew all of it.

OK, he reckoned, so Andrews – and he still wanted to talk to her about the missing money since she had been screwing one of the Harling's underlings, Coren – was about to visit the States, and that was most decidedly his territory. He would find out what her exact plans were, where she would be and when. It might – no: almost certainly would – be a lot easier getting to her in America than on her home ground of Belfast.

For the moment, then, he would postpone facing the reporter and concentrate on what to do about his more immediate problem: that of Meredith.

Once again he replayed in his mind the events of the morning and arrived at the same conclusion: he wasn't going to get the information he needed from her. Plain and simple, she was in such bad shape that she could not remember where the money was. She had probably had to write down the vital codes and account numbers somewhere and the chances of her remembering where the somewhere was were zilch.

And, turning back to Andrews, had Coren – he couldn't recall his surname – even told her about the money? The way things were falling apart he doubted it.

He got up and in the bathroom splashed cold water on his face, staring at himself in the mirror. His trip was quickly turning into a cartload of horse manure.

He changed his shirt, tucked the newspaper into his jacket pocket and on the way from the room he grabbed the In Your Pocket guide-book: might as well look like a tourist.

He returned to the City Hall grounds and found a seat. It was an afternoon of bright sunshine and a blue, cloudless sky. The office girls were finishing their lunches on the clipped lawns around the statues of city worthies and making their way back to their filing cabinets and computer desks.

Only the genuine tourists were left to pose and chatter in front of the building. It reminded him of several State Capitol buildings across the United States with its big green dome. Jesus, he thought with a rare smile, he was beginning to like, actually like, Belfast. Well, at least not to dismiss it as a complete waste of space ... the dames were neat, he conceded. The In Your Pocket guide certainly painted it in glowing terms.

Rachel hurried from the News Letter and crossed Donegall Square South towards the City Hall. As she walked along the path at the front of the building she noticed the man sitting on his own reading the newspaper. A brief think-I've-seen-him-before moment struck her and departed almost immediately.

Marvin's mobile tinkled and he took it from his pocket and flicked it open.

"It's Maguire," the voice said before he could speak, "We have a problem. I'll send Dermot to pick you up. Where are you?"

"At the City Hall. What's the problem?"

"Not on the 'phone. Meet him at the front gate in15 minutes."

Maguire hung up before Marvin could press him on the problem. A problem he did not need. What the hell was going on?

He walked to the gates, dumping the newspaper in a litter-bin along the path. He stood at the gates as a party of Japanese giggled and posed, one by one, for photographs to prove that they had been in Belfast. Why did Japanese tourists do that? They couldn't take a group picture, no matter how large their party they all had to have individual shots of themselves standing in front of a building or a statue or whatever.

A clock on one of the buildings at the corner of Donegall Square North and Donegall Place registered 2.35pm as Dermot pulled in from the flowing traffic. Marvin got into the back of the car. It still stank of cigarettes and cloying sweat. It also smelled of something else: fear, that was it, fear.

"What's the problem?"

Dermot sneaked a quick glance in the rear-view mirror and shrugged: "Best let Maguire fill you in."

In silence, worried silence on Marvin's part, they followed the same route as that morning and the same routine when they reached the safe house: stopping several doors beyond the house, taking the alley behind the houses to the wooden yard door, knocking on it, being ushered into the yard and into the kitchen.

Marvin hoped they varied their routines more frequently than once every six months, but kept the thought to himself.

The driver – Sean – was leaning against the door frame leading to the hallway: "Maguire wants to see you, he's in the parlour."

Marvin assumed that was the front room downstairs, one he had not yet been in. He pushed past the driver and into the room.

It was neat and spotlessly clean. There was a low, red-coloured leather sofa and two easy chairs making up the set. A glass-topped coffee-table stood on a white, fluffy, sheep-shaped rug – it could even have been a real sheep hide – and underneath was an oatmeal corded carpet. There was a small, black metal fireplace with unlit logs and several large coloured candles on the hearth tiles. On the walls were more large prints of the Irish countryside and above the fireplace was a team photograph of players in green and white-striped shirts, with a green and white woollen scarf draped around it. It meant nothing to Marvin, the New York Mets it wasn't.

He had spoken on a couple of occasions to Maguire – he had no idea what his first name was – but had never met him. Marvin looked at the man sitting on the sofa by the window.

He wasn't what Marvin had expected, even if he had not given it much thought. The man was slim and had a mop of unruly black hair parted in the middle. He wore thin-rimmed steel glasses and looked like somebody who had auditioned for the role of Harry Potter and hadn't bothered changing afterwards. He looked like a late-teen college nerd.

Maguire silently indicated one of the chairs, deliberately Marvin took the other one.   Maguire allowed a faint, knowing smile to flit across his lips. OK, he thought, we'll have the pissing, mine-is-bigger-than-yours contest and then we'll get down to business.

Marvin arranged the cushions behind his back and settled into the chair.

"So, what's the problem?"

Maguire thought for a moment, then said: "We've lost the woman."

Marvin shot out of the chair: "What? You let her escape, let her fucking walk out? She was fucking naked … did one of the dickheads nip out and buy her a new outfit?"

Maguire waited quietly for the outburst to subside.

"Sit down, and let me finish," he said calmly, "No, she didn't escape … naked or otherwise. She's upstairs … she's dead."

Marvin remained seated this time. He rubbed a hand over his eyes before fixing his gaze across the room.

"OK, so tell me what happened."

"About an hour after you left," Maguire began, "I got a frantic 'phone call from Dermot. He said you had told them nobody was to watch over her, so they stayed downstairs …" He was trying to spread the blame.

"And?"

"And they did. At least he thought that's what happened. Around 1:30 he and Sean went up to the main road to get a couple of fish suppers and when they came back Arty, the kid you threw down the stairs, was throwing his guts up in the kitchen. He'd gone up to have a look at her and …"

"And the fucker couldn't keep his hands off her …"

"We don't know for certain that's what happened."

"I know," Marvin said, "I know that's what happened. The little shit went for a quick grope …"

Maguire held his hand up to stall another rant: "Maybe, maybe not. All I know is that as soon as I got Dermot's call I came here and checked it out. She was slumped over in the chair, and she was dead."

Marvin lashed out at the table: "Great, just fucking wonderful. I needed her alive … the New York people aren't going to like any of this. A right cock-up you've made of it."

"It's unfortunate …"

Marvin snorted.

" … unfortunate," Maguire continued, "but now we have an additional problem, you understand? You probably haven't been listening to the news, but they're out looking for her. What we now have to do is get rid of the body."

"And how do you propose to do that?"

"Let's just say we're not exactly inexperienced in that department. Tonight we'll take her well away from here and dispose of her. Nobody will ever find her."

"Where? I want to know where, exactly, you'll be dumping her. I need to report back to New York."

Maguire reached down to the side of the sofa and lifted a folded map of Northern Ireland. He spread it open on the coffee-table, beckoning Marvin to come closer.

"When it's dark," Maguire said, "we'll take her out to the car, nobody will be around at that time and if they are they'll know to turn the other way, you understand me? Good, I'll have Dermot …"

"And the kid, what's his name, Alfred?"

"Arty, you mean Arty?"

"Yeah, him. I want him along too. And I'm going as well. I want to make sure the Hole-in-the-Wall Gang don't leave her in the middle of Royal Avenue."

Maguire thought for a moment, but Marvin tapped the map.

"No thinking to do about it. I'm going too, period. Now where are we going? Show me."

Maguire explained the plan, traced his finger along a line leading from Belfast to the West of Northern Ireland, to where County Fermanagh ran up against County Donegal.

"It's a long way, bit of a risk going that far."

Maguire shook his head and pointed to a long stretch of water either side of a town Marvin saw was Enniskillen: "Nowhere is ever too far away in the Six Counties. Anyway, it's been done before, believe me. It'll be OK. We've used Lough Erne, this is Lough Erne, before. There are plenty of small islands dotted about the Lough, we know them, we've used them before."

"How long will it take us to get there?"

"They'll leave around 1.15am and be there around 3.30, 3.45 tops. I'll make arrangements for a boat to be waiting to take you to the island we've selected."

"OK," Marvin said, adding after some thought, "Show me how

to get to Enniskillen."

"But you're going with them, aren't you?"

"No, I have a lot to do so I'll make my own way to Enniskillen and hook up with them there. Just show me on the map the quickest way there and arrange some place where I can meet them, OK?"

"Sure, if that's what you want," Maguire waved him around to the same side of the table and drew in the route to Enniskillen, "It's simple enough, you hit the M1 here and just follow it as far as it goes to this roundabout. From there you go through these wee towns, Augher, Clogher, Fivemiletown, and bingo you reach Enniskillen. At that time of the night you should have no trouble making it in good time, couple of hours tops.

"Just before you get to Enniskillen, about a mile out, on the left, there's a big hotel complex, the Killyhevlin: Dermot and Arty will meet you on the main road running past the hotel, say at 3.15, and take you to the boat. Got that?"

"Yeah," Marvin said, "Tell them to be careful, I don't want them arriving with a convoy of cop cars in tow. They've fucked this up enough, it ends here. Oh, and one last thing: expect a call from New York. Have you got that?"

He had one more request to make: "Do me a favour, I'll call you about it in a couple of days. The News Letter is advertising some Stateside trip one of their reporters, Rachel Andrews, is making at the end of the month. See if you can get a schedule ... like if she'll be in New York, where she'll be staying and when. How she'll be travelling around the States. That sort of thing. Think you can do that without buggering it up?"

"Yes. We have a couple of contacts in the 'paper, shouldn't be too much of a problem. I'll get everything I can about her trip."

Marvin – no, he didn't want to see Meredith: if she's dead, she's dead and of no further use to him - left the house and re-traced the way back through the jungle of streets to the Falls Road. He waited for a bus and arrived back at the hotel half-an-hour later, on the way stopping to purchase a large vacuum flask and an Ordinance Survey map of Northern Ireland.

He asked reception to hire him a car, put in a call to New York and listened to the instructions. He packed, went downstairs and paid his bill. He returned to his room, had a shower, changed his clothes and ordered a meal from room service. He had the rest of the evening to relax and await the journey West.

If Maguire got the Andrews' schedule he could catch up with her in New York. The situation was desperate but not hopeless.

He finished the meal and left the hotel to pick up the hire car, parking it in a side street behind St Anne's Cathedral. Back at the hotel he checked out, At 10pm he used the coffee packs in his room and boiled the kettle. He filled the flask with strong, sweet, black coffee and slipped it into his bag. He walked from the hotel, crossed Waring Street and went up the cobbled Hill Street with its many fashionable cafes and restaurants.

At the car he removed the flask and put the bag on the back seat. He studied the map and worked out the route to Enniskillen.

Like any good General on the eve of a battle he had decided to arrive at the battlefield early and select the best vantage point. He would make his leisurely way to Enniskillen, find the hotel and get a feel of the surrounding landscape. As yet, of course, he had no idea where the island was, how far from shore it would be, what sort of boat they would be using … but he figured it would not require a long journey to reach it since what they planned to do required darkness. After that: well, he knew what he had to do.

Traffic was light out of Belfast, though he had difficulty working out how to get onto the M1 since there appeared to be major roadworks all along the way. He had to weave in and out between long rows of red-topped plastic bollards before finding the Motorway itself. But once on it he made good progress.

Darkness was chasing the sun from the sky with the promise of a pale full moon in a cloudy sky. Perfect conditions for the task ahead.

Along the M1 he pulled off to a slip road and poured himself a beaker of coffee. It had not been a successful trip, he reflected, not successful at all. He had come to get information from Meredith Harling and now she was dead. He conceded that he probably would not have obtained the information anyway, even had she lived.

There was still the possibility that the reporter had what he needed, and she was heading to America, to his backyard. That, he felt, was a decided plus. All in the future, he told himself as he started the car and rejoined the Motorway West.

He hit the Ballygawley Roundabout and followed the signs to Enniskillen, passing through the slumbering small towns Maguire had pointed out: Augher, Clougher, Fivemiletown. A couple of trucks passed him on their way East towards Belfast but apart from that his was the only vehicle on the road.

He came to the Killyhevlin, a large complex at the side of a lake, Marvin assumed it was the Erne, and drove past it. He stopped the car, reversed into a narrow lane and drove back past the hotel. He was looking for somewhere to park the car.

He found another narrow lane shaded by trees and drove slowly along it until he came to a clearing. He eased the car into the clearing, pointing it in the direction of the main road. He got out to stretch his legs. The night was still warm, the only sound the rustling of the leaves overhead. Off to his right he detected the sound of water lapping the shore. Back at the car he clicked his seat back, poured another coffee and punched on the radio. He had plenty of time, he settled in for a sleep.

The buzz of his watch alarm roused him. He stretched and rubbed the sleep from his eyes. He tried another coffee but it was now luke-warm and bitter. He checked his watch, it was 2.30. He reached across the seat and lifted over his bag, searching for his toilet-bag. He took out a toothbrush and from the door side-pocket a bottle of still water. He brushed his teeth and swilled water around his mouth. He splashed some on his face and felt alive enough to get out and wait for the car from Belfast.

Thankfully it was a mild night. He reached the main road, walked towards the hotel and sat on the verge, hoping no passing car would wonder why a man was sitting at the side of the road in the middle of the night. Luckily, no vehicles passed.

They arrived dead on 3.15. They drew up alongside him and he got in.

"Been waiting long?" Dermot asked.

"No, just got here. So where are we going?"

"Just the other side of the town. Shouldn't take long."

"Good," Marvin said, "I trust you remembered to bring the package."

"Yeah, it's in the boot."

They drove through Enniskillen and Marvin picked up signs to Belleek and Donegal. On a lonely stretch of the twisting road they turned right into a lane and bounced along the ruts. Ahead, he could see lake water shimmering in the moonlight.

"We're here," Dermot said, stopping the car and getting out. Arty, who had remained silent throughout the short journey, followed.

"Go get the boat," Dermot told him and he took off into the trees at the water's edge. He returned presently to confirm that the boat was all ready.

"Help me get the bitch out," Dermot said, pulling the boot open.

Marvin stood at the side of the car and watched as they struggled with the body. It was wrapped in black plastic bin-liners. They carried it down the lane and into the trees to an inflatable with an engine at the stern. They cursed as they tried to heave the body onto the boat.

"You coming along?" Dermot asked.

"No, I'll leave it up to you. I don't want to know where you bury her, just do it. I'll wait here. Don't take all night. Now get going."

They scrambled into the inflatable and Dermot pushed it away from the bank with a long paddle. The boat glided silently into the lake and Marvin watched as Arty chugged the engine into life. It spluttered and churned the dark waters and disappeared into the centre of the lake towards a small, tree-covered island.

Marvin sat on the bonnet of the car listening to what he reckoned was the deafening throb of the boat engine, loud enough to have the entire neighbourhood up and at its windows.

Just over 30 minutes later he heard the boat returning. Dermot steered it into the bank, Arty jumped out and secured it to a tree.

"The job's a good one," Dermot said when they got to the car, "I'll run you back to the hotel."

"That won't be necessary," Marvin said, "I'll see my own way back."

He shot them and pulled their bodies deep into the bushes at the side of the lane. He drove their car back through Enniskillen to the hotel, down the lane past his own car and unscrewed the top of the petrol tank. He stuffed his handkerchief into the opening and lit it, making sure it would catch fire. He ran back to his car and drove to the main road. From behind him he heard the whump and saw a bright orange flash light up the trees.

He crossed the border into Monaghan and headed for Dublin.

NINE

ONE morning, having spent so many nights of heartache and anguish, you waken up and it simply doesn't matter any more. It is as if a dark and menacing cloud that has blotted out the sun for as long as you could remember is suddenly blown away and all that was causing the sadness and the bitterness and the tears and the denial is no longer of any significance ... whatsoever.

And the pretending then becomes a delicious game. You play your role with magnificent relish; the smiles, the embraces, the kisses, even the sex, come easily because they no longer register. They are merely movements in the dance of time ... one lightly-taken step followed by another, faultlessly performed so that there is no stumbling, no hesitation, nothing at all to suggest that the music has long ceased.

And Delta, with a strength she never realised she possessed, played her role to perfection: the smiles, the embraces, the kisses, even the sex.

She realised she had been foolish to go to Glenwood Springs, so foolish that she could now laugh at it. That frantic rush to confirm what she already knew, the wild – mad – plans that had tumbled through her mind, the realisation that she would be incapable of exacting the revenge she sought. Not there, in Glenwood Springs, but elsewhere ... certainly elsewhere.

She continued to accompany Jackson to their many social events, continued to be photographed for the newspapers and magazines, continued her enthusiastic support of him, continued playing the adoring co-star in the drama of the Golden Couple.

She even continued making love to him – no, it was no longer love, it was sex ... and she was always supreme at sex – and balancing their unreality with reality.

And one morning the curtain rose on the second act of the drama. Jackson, on his own this time, took the company jet to Montana where Octagon was about to launch a new magazine. He had asked if she wanted to accompany him but she reluctantly explained that she had several meetings to attend for several of her charities.

After Jackson had left for the airport Delta showered and drove into downtown Denver, though for this particular meeting charity was the last thing on her mind.

She parked in the underground lot at Writers' Square in the centre of the city and walked across 15th Street to Larimer Street in the old, historic, restored section of Denver.

She entered the Tryst Lounge – she smiled at the delicious irony of the name – and took a table at the back. She sat amid the flickering candles casting dancing shadows on the red walls and sipped a tangy fruit cocktail.

Shortly after, she saw the man enter the lounge, look around and nod towards her. He could not have missed her – they had, anyway, met before – since it was too early in the day for the bright, chattering young things the Tryst was famous for. He bought a vodka and soda and brought it to her table.

"Mrs Wellman," he said, settling in the seat opposite her, "You said on the 'phone that you had another job for me ..."

The man, whom she knew only as Collins, was the private detective she had hired to get information on Jackson's affair. He would not have looked out-of-place or miscast as a TV PI; it was as though he had watched too many such shows and decided that he was what private eyes were supposed to look like: overweight, red-faced, sweating, exuding BO and the cloying smell of cheap cigars and even cheaper cologne. She half expected to see the wallpaper begin to curl at the corners and peel off. For added effect, he was dressed in a cheap, crumpled linen suit stained at the arm-pits.

He was, she figured, perfect.

"Yes, Mr Collins," she said, "I think it's more a job you might be able to have done for me, by someone else. If you can arrange it you will, of course, be richly rewarded. It's a job that must never be traced back to me, you understand ... the arrangements I leave entirely in your hands."

He cupped the vodka in his hands and looked at her.

"If I get your drift, Mrs Wellman," he said after some thought, "you would like a problem disposed of."

She nodded.

"Yes, that's exactly it. Can you take care of it?"

"Well, yes, I can have it taken care of. I have some contacts, quite excellent contacts, who deal with such problems. I can certainly make the necessary calls ... but it's the sort of job that doesn't come cheap, you realise that don't you?"

She nodded.

"What would the fee be?" she asked.

He thought for a moment then took from his pocket a small notebook and pen. She watched as he scribbled down several sums of money and then slid them across the table. She smoothed the torn page with her long fingers and scrutinised the figures.

She looked up: "That seems to be satisfactory. So I can leave the arrangements up to you ... and there will be absolutely no connection leading back to me?"

"I can guarantee that. I'll make the call and set it up for you. I know the party you wish to have removed but I need a photograph to send to my contact ..."

Delta opened her bag and took out a photograph, sliding it across the table. He looked at it and put it into his pocket.

"There is also the matter of when and where the, er, the removal is to take place."

She considered this and said: "Yes, I understand. I don't want it to take place here in Denver, too close to home I think. The parties will doubtless find a way of being out of Colorado in the near future, it would be better if your contact met them then. I will let you know when and where."

He nodded: "And it's just the one party you need removed?"

"Yes, just the one. Have your contact remove the bitch ... I have other plans for my husband."

He finished his drink and pushed himself from the table. He stood over her: "I'll call you in a couple of days, let you know about the financial arrangements. You'll be in touch about the most suitable location?"

Delta nodded and he left. She waved at the waitress and pointed to her glass.

She thought a spot of dedicated retail therapy would round off the afternoon.

Rachel checked the story she had just written for her week-end column: working mothers and how they cope. She was a working single and found coping difficult but here she was reading about the two, energetic mothers who ran a small local tourist magazine, kept their houses spotless, cooked magnificent meals, entertained their friends lavishly and threw in, for good measure, some charity work. Even as she had been interviewing them she could have strangled them.

She made a couple of changes, checked a couple of quotes from her notebook and sent it across to the subs. It was 5.30pm.

She shut down her computer and walked across to the News Desk to see if there was anything needed doing, hoping there wasn't. There wasn't. She returned to her desk and 'phoned Jayne at the BBC. It took so long for an answer that she reckoned it would have been quicker walking the short distance between the News Letter and Broadcasting House.

"Hi, it's me," she said when the receptionist finally tracked Jayne down, "Fancy a swift half? We can pick up some pizza and go over our plans for next week."

"God, yes," Jayne said, "I'm counting the minutes, can't believe we'll be in the good old US of A in a week's time. I keep waiting for one of the suits here to tell me they've changed their minds, that it was just a bit of a giggle."

"Listen, lady, even if they do we're still going. I'm all over the 'paper warning readers about it and Karen appears to have cleaned out her and daddy's bank accounts to subsidise the trip. So, we're going, end of story."

"And not just the 'paper," Jayne said, "I've had a word with the producer of Alan Simpson's afternoon Radio Ulster show and, guess what, they want a regular down-the-line chat with you. Since I'm just an obscure producer and you're a big-name columnist it's you they want. It'll earn you a few bob for your return."

"That's terrific, it'll go towards paying Karen back. Drinks and pizza on me, then."

"OK, give me half-an-hour and I'll meet you in Robinsons."

Several swift halves and a pizza later, they were in Rachel's apartment working through their itinerary.

Rachel would fly from Dublin to New York, Jayne from Dublin to Boston. They would spend three days in their respective cities, get the Amtrak Lake Shore Limited – one leg of the service left Manhattan, the other Boston – and meet up at Albany-Rensselaer when the two trains came together. From there it was an overnight run into Chicago and a couple of hours wait for the three-day-two night California Zephyr to San Fransisco. Four days in the City by the Bay before they left their hearts and caught the Coast Starlight to Los Angeles. Four days there doing the tourist rounds of Disneyland, Universal Studios, Beverly Hills – Rodeo Drive, most certainly Rodeo Drive with all those mouth-watering shops – and the bronzed hunks at Muscle Beach and down to the end of the line in San Diego: coast-to-coast. Then it would be back to LA and the flight home. Four glorious weeks … roll on!

Karen had already spoken to the nice people at the Regency in Park Avenue and booked a room for Rachel. Jayne had booked a room in the Boston Harbor Hotel at Bowe's Wharf.

Roll on!

"What about the contacts for while you're in the Big Apple?" Jayne wanted to know. They had arranged the separate starts to their trip to allow Jayne to meet with the Amtrak people in Boston to discuss her proposed radio documentary series about taking the railway routes from the Atlantic to the Pacific while the News Letter had stipulated that as part of Rachel's deal for the time off her journey should begin in New York.

It also stipulated that she send back a regular supply of features – interviews with Northern Irish exiles she met along the way, general lifestyle interest features and a weekly travelogue.

"Well," Rachel said, getting up from the sofa to bring back a leather writing-case with a large yellow legal notepad, "the PSNI Press people put me in touch with the NYPD and they said they'd find me a genuine Irish – hopefully Northern Irish – cop to interview," she flicked through the notepad, "and there's a Brian Friel play opening off-Broadway with a couple of Dublin actors heading the cast, so I've e-mailed them and lined up an interview.

"There's a woman who was born in Cookstown who works for a Madison Avenue PR outfit and a chef from Larne who works in a restaurant in Manhattan. That's for starters, who knows what else I'll come across once I get there."

"Sounds like you'll be busy. Just make sure you have enough free time to enjoy yourself. This may be a working trip but I intend to have a good time," Jayne warned.

"I can't believe we're really going, can you?" Rachel said, "I know everybody seems to fly over to New York and Boston as easily as taking the bus to Bangor, but to actually go ourselves and then take in Chicago, San Fransisco, Los Angeles, Hollywood and San Diego and everything in between ... "

"Easy old thing, you'll do yourself an embarrassment!"

They fell about hugging each other and laughing.

Roll on!

Marvin returned to his Murray Hill apartment in Manhattan and slept for 20 hours straight. After he awoke and had a cold shower he went out to his favourite corner shop – owned by a long-resident Korean family – and purchased coffee, milk, fresh juice and several bags of food.

In the apartment he brewed a coffee and made a 'phone call. What surprised him when he had finished the call was not that Maguire had, as promised, managed to obtain the details of Rachel's trip to America – and yes, she would be staying for several days in New York – but that he had not once mentioned the missing Dermot and Arty. It was as if Maguire had decided they had never existed, their disappearance merely a minor glitch of no importance.

In the afternoon he grabbed a cab and went to the Empire State Building, not to thrill at the view of Manhattan from the Statue of Liberty to Grand Central Park and beyond but to meet one of the associates. On the observation deck he stood and scanned the horizon through one of the mounted binoculars and waited for a man to move through the crowd of jostling, pointing tourists towards him.

The man leaned on the parapet: "They made a bloody mess of things in Belfast."

Marvin continued to sweep the binoculars across the city.

"Yes, but it's been taken care of," he said, "She wasn't going to give us what we wanted without a struggle but I believe I was getting there ... until ..."

The man, he decided, did not need to know the entire truth, which was fine with Marvin since he wasn't going to tell it.

"So how do we retrieve the situation? We're being pressed for a result."

Marvin gave it some thought: "We got a break. It might be just what we need. You remember the newspaper reporter, Rachel Andrews, who covered a lot of the story about the Tabernacle ... well, she was screwing Coren whatever-his-name-was and there's a chance he might, just might, have let something slip about the money. It's a long shot, I know ... but the break is she's coming here, to NYC, next week. I think I'll arrange a meeting with her, see what she knows."

The man nodded: "Good, that's worth the effort. I'll leave the fine points to you. Good work."

Marvin made big with reading the building's guidebook he had collected earlier and the man slipped quietly into the crowd and disappeared.

TEN

IF Karen asked one more time if she had finished her packing – she hadn't even started – and if she had checked that her passport was in order and if she had been to the bank and got her traveller's cheques and Dollars and if she had her tickets in a safe place and if she knew who to call in case of an emergency, Rachel would not be held responsible for her actions.

She had gone to the house in Lisburn to deliver Kelly, her Manx cat, and to leave a spare set of keys to her apartment. She and Karen were sitting at the table on the patio at the front of the house, having an anything-but-calming glass of wine and enjoying the hot sunshine. Kelly was playfully scampering after butterflies on the long sweep of lawn that led to the main road, scampering fruitlessly since he never, ever actually caught one. The chase was everything.

"Well, darling," Karen said, "what a big adventure, eh? Off to America … when do you leave?"

"Day after tomorrow. We'll drive down to Dublin tomorrow, stay in a B&B near the airport and I fly to New York in the morning and Jayne goes to Boston that afternoon."

"That's nice," Karen said, and Rachel had the distinct feeling she had lost her step-mother at the "Day after …" bit.

"And everything is organised?"

"Yes, everything," Rachel fibbed, knowing that she would have to drive back to Belfast and spend the evening and the following morning frantically packing, checking her passport, getting her cheques and money from the bank, sorting out her tickets, "It's really only a holiday to the USA, you know, millions of people do it every year. It's not a dangerous expedition up the Amazon in search of a mysterious lost civilisation … you just have to get on a 'plane at Dublin and five or six hours later get off it in New York. I think I can manage to do that."

"That's nice," Karen said.

Rachel smiled and rolled her eyes.

"Willie will certainly enjoy his little holiday," Karen said. Rachel did not bother to correct her.

The departure the following afternoon turned out to be exactly like the start of a dangerous expedition, falling just short of a brass band, flags and bunting, fireworks and speeches.

Karen, Sandi and Brian Leonard were at Rachel's apartment for the send-off. Jayne had driven over from her own flat and they were loading Rachel's car with the luggage – far too much luggage, Brian reckoned – since she and Jayne had tossed to see whose car they would use to get to Dublin.

Everybody hugged – a small ritual Brian quite enjoyed – and waved – Rachel hoped nobody would actually be gross enough to cry: it was only a holiday for goodness sake – and they drove out of the apartment complex and headed for the M1 and Dublin.

"Why do I have this niggling feeling that I've left something behind?" Jayne wondered.

"It happens to all of us, it's part of the great mystery of travel," Rachel assured her, "There was a photographer on the News Letter who once went to cover a big football match … without his camera."

"You have a warped way of easing my anxiety. Oh well, if I've forgotten to pack my knickers I can always buy some in Boston."

"I intend to buy a lot of things everywhere we stop. Karen's given me a long list of absolutely-must-visit boutiques around Manhattan, it would be churlish of me not to pay them a visit. And let's not even think of not doing Rodeo Drive shop by shop."

Jayne shuddered and laughed: "Let's certainly not."

Just beyond Drogheda they pulled off the main road and found a pub-restaurant. They sat in the garden behind the whitewashed building and ordered tea and a plate of home-made wheaten bread with cheese.

"Where are we staying tonight?" Rachel asked. Jayne had made the arrangements.

"Caroline in the press office recommended it," Jayne said, "It's three miles from the airport, in a little village called Castleton-something, or something-castleton. We're booked into Rosedale House, all Laura Ashley, Mansion polish and breakfasts that would fell a horse, so Caroline says."

"Sounds ideal."

They resumed their journey and made Castleton – no something either end, just plain Castleton – shortly after 5.30 and were shown to their room. It had two bouncy single-beds, fresh flowers, all Laura Ashley and Mansion polish.

They washed away the journey, had a light dinner – that would also have felled a horse – and decided to explore the village, a task that consumed all of ten minutes since Castleton consisted of a couple of shops, a row of brightly-coloured cottages, a large, Gothic chapel, a small Church of Ireland building that looked positively embarrassed to be seen in public and four pubs. Castleton knew how to gets the priorities right, the girls decided.

And since they decided it would be ungracious of them not to pay a visit they picked one – O'Malley's, with its green-painted, flower-decked exterior and friendly chatter and laughter wafting from the front door – and entered.

They felt like the Most Feared Gunmen in the Old West striding into a saloon for there was a brief hush and the scrutiny of interested eyes before the chatter resumed. They found a table and Rachel weaved her way to the bar to buy two pints of Guinness.

"God, what induced you to buy that?" Jayne asked when Rachel had balanced the drink back through the crowd.

"It was the only thing I could think of. Anyway, haven't you heard Guinness is good for you? Doctors recommend it."

"I've never come across a doctor who recommended strong drink. They drink it themselves but tell you to lay off it. Still, when in Castleton," Jayne raised her glass, "Still, cheers … here's to an unforgettable trip."

"I'll drink to that."

In the corner of the bar a small band threw itself into an energetic medley of reels and jigs and a man dressed in what looked like the stage costume of a farmer joined in with a song, following it with a rambling and funny story about a local ghost and the wee folk.

Just what the tourists loved about Aul' Oirland.

"He's probably the local doctor," Jayne said, "Tomorrow we'll see him racing around town in his Mercedes."

"So cynical for one so young," Rachel chided her friend with a giggle.

They returned eventually and unsteadily to Rosedale House,

having beaten off a stream of offers for more drink from the locals, though Jayne gave in and joined in a rowdy jig. They collapsed into the beds, ready for what America had to offer.

Manhattan morning and Marvin liked his served as a plain omelette with crisp bacon strips on the side. The one thing he missed about Northern Ireland was the real bacon, not the watery slices Americans called bacon. Throw in a couple of slices of potato bread or – and – a fried soda and you had the makings of a good breakfast. He liked it washed down with sweet, black coffee. Herman's Mid-Town Diner never disappointed.

He leafed through a copy of the New Yorker and watched the crowds on the busy avenue outside.

It was time, once again, to scout the terrain, to search out, as it were, the high ground. From what Maguire had told him, Andrews would be checking into the Regency on Park Avenue the following afternoon so he figured he had better take a look for himself.

He left the Diner and at the kerb held up his hand until a yellow cab weaved through the traffic and drew up in front of him. He got in and told the driver to take him to the hotel at 540 Park Avenue and 61st Street. The driver, surprisingly a native New Yorker, not too many of that endangered species plying their trade, tried some chatty conversation but gave up in the face of Marvin's determined silence.

The hotel – famous, so it claimed, as the home of the power breakfast – was on a tree-lined street near Central Park, a couple of blocks from the Fifth and Madison Avenue shops.

He paid the cabbie and walked into the hotel, nodding a greeting to the uniformed, saluting doorman who looked like he'd just come from the crowd scene in a Broadway performance of a Franz Lehar operetta.

He covered his brief recce by walking to the reception desk and asking for a guest he knew didn't exist. He apologised for his mistake, had a look around and walked back to the street. The lobby contained several good private areas where, if necessary, he could wait until the reporter showed.

He also wondered, since the hotel was up-market, how she could afford to stay in it. Was she using some of the missing money, he wondered? Maybe she did know where it was stashed away.

Welcome to the Big Apple, Miss Andrews ... see you soon.

The girls had the famous Rosedale breakfast and staggered to the car, staggered both from the aftermath of the previous night's visit to O'Malley's and from the mammoth plates of eggs, soda, potato-bread, bacon, sausages, tomatoes, mushrooms and buttered wheaten bread they had demolished. Enough, Rachel suggested, to sustain them until they reached Chicago at least.

They drove the couple of miles to Dublin Airport, parked in a far corner of the long-term park, found a couple of conveniently abandoned carts and trundled them into the Departures area, checked in for their flights and did a quick tour of the shops, selecting several magazines.

It was eight in the morning since Rachel's Aer Lingus flight to Kennedy was at 10.30 and Jayne's to Boston at 2.30.

Karen had paid for them to relax in the Anna Livia Departure Lounge where they found a quiet corner. They fetched tea and sank back into the comfortable chairs.

The friendly, helpful receptionist came for Rachel, gave her the boarding pass and moved on to round up the other New York passengers.

The girls stood and hugged as the receptionist returned to escort them all to the gate.

"Now don't get into any trouble on the flight," Jayne warned, "Save it all for when we meet up."

"It's really exciting, isn't it?" Rachel said, picking up her travel-bag and laptop, "I wonder what mad adventures lie ahead, eh? OK, I'm off … I'll give you a call later tonight to see you've arrived safely and I'll see you at Albany in four day's time. Check your knickers."

They giggled and hugged again and Jayne watched her friend lead the charge from the Lounge.

Delta played the game to perfection, she had become an expert at pretending. She even found herself quite relishing the deception. How wonderfully delicious it all was.

And, even better, she discovered that Jackson was going to Chicago on the company jet for another important, mustn't-miss business meeting. And, of course, Wendy was to accompany him. Delta did not even bother to ask, in case of emergencies, where he would be staying since she had already found out. She was getting good at finding out things. She had the dates, the destination … all she now needed was a 'phone call.

When Jackson had left for the office, Delta went into the garden and dialled Collins with the details.

"OK, I'll let my contact know," Collins told her, "He's already been sent the photo, he'll take it from there. Lodge the fee in the account I gave you. When the job's complete I'll let you know ... though, of course, you'll probably know yourself."

"And ..."

"Don't worry, nothing can be traced back to you."

Delta drove into Denver and from her bank account drew out $50,000 in cash. Such a sum hardly registered ... she was, after all, Delta Dubette-Wellman of Octagon Enterprises. If the bank gave it any thought at all they would assume it was for yet another of Delta's bursaries. It was something she did regularly.

She walked to another bank and deposited the money in an account in the name of Colorado Import-Export.

ELEVEN

JAYNE stretched out in her quiet corner of the Anna Livia Lounge and flicked through a magazine. She fell into a snooze and when she jolted back to life, wondering where on earth she was, it was 11.15am and she felt peckish, in spite of the gargantuan breakfast.

She asked the receptionist if she could leave her travelling-bag and laptop while she went to one of the airport restaurants for a quick early lunch. The girl took the bag and computer and put them into a small room behind her desk.

The airport was bustling with passengers departing, arriving, seeing off and welcoming. She walked around the various cafes and restaurants, most of them packed with families, and selected a sea food bar. She collected a tray, asked for a Haddock in Guinness batter with creamed potatoes and garden peas, she got a glass of cold milk, slid the food to the girl at the cash register and, glancing around, saw a couple leaving a table. She hurried over to it.

She lingered for 45 minutes and then walked to the clicking boards to check on her Boston flight. She returned to the Lounge and picked up her bag and laptop to await the call for the 'plane.

While she waited she filled in the forms the receptionist had given her and slipped them into a side-pocket of the laptop case.

She joined the line of waiting passengers when her seat number was called and walked along the corridor to the 'plane. Inside, she negotiated the obstacle course of people milling about in the aisle and sorting out their luggage. She found her seat towards the front of the 'plane, a window seat. She took out a notebook and several magazines and put her luggage into the overhead bin. She put her cream linen jacket on the middle seat and settled in for the journey.

She was flicking through the in-flight magazine when she heard the voice.

"Excuse me, is this jacket yours?"

She looked up. Wow, she thought as she took in the man smiling down at her. He wore a light, navy-blue suit with a pale blue shirt and striped tie. He wore steel-rimmed glasses and his sandy hair flopped over his brow. He had one of those smiles a lady never forgets.

Suddenly flustered at being caught looking at him, Jayne grabbed the jacket. He reached across and took it from her, folding it carefully and indicating whether he should put it in the bin.

Jayne nodded, foolishly feeling her mouth go dry. Catch yourself on, for dear sake. Get a life, lady.

He removed his own jacket and stretched to put it alongside hers before sitting down and clicking on his safety belt. While he was doing this Jayne realised she had been watching his every move.

Usually when she took a flight the best looking man always walked past her seat to sit next to some stunning blonde … and usually she got an overweight and sweating toilet-roll salesman who snored throughout the journey and ended up with his bald head lolling on her shoulder with drool dribbling down his chin.

OK, slight exaggeration there but you get the gist. She offered a prayer that the empty seat between them wasn't waiting for the toilet-roll salesman.

"I'm Brad Carey, by the way," the man said, reaching over to shake her hand.

He had a Boston accent, Jayne noted as she croaked back that she was Jayne McGregor. She furtively chewed her tongue to get some moisture into her mouth.

"You off to Boston … well, of course you are, daft question," Brad said, smiling, "I mean are you staying in Boston or moving on?"

"Yes, on both counts. I'll be staying in Boston for several days and then I'm taking the train across the States, to San Diego." "Well, I'm impressed. We Yanks seem to have forgotten we still run trains. I haven't been on a train for years. Actually, I can't remember ever being on one. That's quite a trip you have lined up, I'm envious. I take it the train trip is just for fun."

"Well, again, yes and no," Jayne said.

She did not realise they had already roared down the runway and lifted off into the clouds as she explained about her job, the potential Amtrak project for the BBC, about her friend Rachel who had left that morning for New York, about their reunion in Albany … indeed, she did not realise she was flying at all.

"Oh dear," she said when she had finished, "I've been rambling, haven't I?"

Brad laughed: "Not at all, it sounds terrific. Do you think the BBC will take the series?"

"Well, only if I sell it to them. Let's just say I'm quietly confident. Anyway, I still intend to have a great time."

"You know, it always amazes me when I talk to Europeans. They have been to cities in the States I've never even heard of. Americans do tend to be insular … if you live in DC and World War Three breaks out in Maryland you think it hardly matters to you, you'll be lucky if a DC newspaper even bothers to mention it.

"Hold on, I just remembered something might help you with Amtrak. A colleague in the office did some legal work for Amtrak when they were extending the line from Boston up to Portland, Maine. He worked for the people in Washington, I'm sure he has lots of useful contacts. I'll talk to him about it."

"That would be useful, I know the main office is in Washington, I've already been in contact with their media people, but I needed to talk to the people at the start of the journey. You live in Boston?" Jayne asked.

"Just outside it, in a little New England town. It's all picket fences, white wooden churches. Very twee and picture-postcardy, but I love it. It's on the coast so I can get in plenty of sailing … I guess I'm a frustrated Captain Ahab. I work in Boston … if you promise not to mention a certain television show I'll tell you what I do for a living …"

Jayne thought for a moment and suddenly smiled: "OK, I claim the first prize … you're a lawyer!"

"Got it in one, sharp lady," Brad said, "I've been doing some business with clients in Dublin and Kilkenny. It's not quite Boston Legal I'm sorry to say, it's all corporate mergers, take-overs, down-sizing, crunching numbers. And my secretary is a 60-year-old grandmother called Agatha Pinkerton. I come over to Ireland two or three times a year, but I've never been in Northern Ireland."

"This is my first visit to Boston. A couple of years ago I was in Florida, but then hasn't everybody been in Florida? I hear Boston is a beautiful city."

"That it is," Brad said, "It's what I call a walking city, it doesn't overwhelm you like a lot of American cities," he thought for a moment, "I'd like to show you around, that is if you don't mind ..."

If I don't mind, Jayne thought, I wouldn't mind like a drowning man wouldn't mind being thrown a lifebelt and a rope.

She gave it a touch of coy reluctance – why sir, you're but a passing stranger – before she nodded: "I'd like that very much ... my very own Boston tour guide!"

"Where are you staying?"

"At the Boston Harbor Hotel. I picked it from Google. It looks quite swanky."

"It's a magnificent hotel, right on the water and just along from Faneuil Marketplace, that's one stop on the Exclusive Carey Tours you'll have to make. And then I'll take you to the Boston Tea Ship and you can throw your own sack of tea overboard ..."

As subtly as she could Jayne glanced at his left hand and, for what it was worth, saw no wedding ring.

"And to Cheers," she added.

"OK, even to Cheers, although the series wasn't actually filmed there, as a lot of people think, the series was just sort-off based on a Boston bar like Cheers. Cheers really began as the Bull and Finch. But, OK, if you like I'll play Norm for you."

"I have meetings most of tomorrow with the Amtrak people but I'm free for the next two days."

Too eager, she chided herself, calm down.

"OK, I'll call you tomorrow afternoon and perhaps we could have dinner. Boston is known as Bean Town but if you don't like beans I might be able to find somewhere else."

"It's a date, then," Jayne felt herself suddenly blushing at what she had said.

They talked all the way across the Atlantic, merely picking at the food the stewardess brought them and hardly even noticing the 'plane land gently at Logan International and trundle to the gate. They sat and allowed the other passengers to file out and Brad took their luggage from the bin.

"Welcome to Boston, Miss McGregor," he said, helping her into the aisle, "I'll meet you after you've gone through immigration and customs, I'll be wearing a red rose and carrying a copy of the Boston Globe, you can't miss me ... I'll be smiling."

When she had negotiated the fierce scrutiny of the new arrivals

Jayne wheeled her case out into the airport lobby.

"My driver is waiting for us outside, we'll drop you off at your hotel," he said, guiding her through the crowd to the front doors. They stopped at the kerbside watching the frantic scramble for taxis and presently a dark Mercedes pulled up in front of them.

"This is it," Brad said, opening the rear door as the driver walked around to put their luggage in the back.

"Did you have a good trip, Mr Carey?" he asked.

"Wonderful, Harry. Ireland is still as green as ever, the whiskey still as potent ... and I've brought you your usual bottle. I trust we're still in business back at the office."

"Looking good when I left," Harry looked at Jayne in his mirror and smiled, "You're staying at the Harbour, Miss McGregor, you'll love it there, one of our finest hotels."

"When Harry says 'our' he means they're one of our clients," Brad said, "as well as being one of the city's best hotels. You made an excellent choice."

At the hotel, while Harry and a bell-hop loaded her luggage on a trolley, Jayne took in the view of two tall-masted sailing ships and rows of bright, sleek luxury yachts lined along the waterfront. She felt the warm sunshine and sniffed the salty tang on the air.

Brad escorted her into the lobby and to the reception desk. He accompanied her in the lift – only now, he told her, it was an elevator and not a lift since Americans don't quite speak the same Queen's English – and while the porter opened her room door and took the trolley inside he turned her towards him, tilted up her chin and kissed her.

"Have a relaxing afternoon, take a stroll along the seafront and I'll call you tomorrow," he said.

Jayne watched him walk along the corridor to the elevator. She went into her room and collapsed on the bed with a happy sigh ... WOW!!!

Harry was leaning against the car looking at the ships.

"That was a very nice colleen, if I may say so."

"That she certainly was," Brad said, getting into the front.

In contrast, Rachel's flight to New York was quite uneventful. She worked her way through the in-flight movie – an indifferent thriller with the compensation of having George Clooney as its star – and most of the in-flight music channels. She dozed fitfully and tried to ignore the annoying little boy who made faces at her over the seat in front. She was in the middle of a three-seat row with a completely silent nun nervously fingering Rosary beads on her right and a completely silent teenage boy on her left, nodding his head in time to the music tinning through his earphones.

She got through the stern J.F. Kennedy 'welcoming committee' – yes, she was here on vacation, no she wasn't a mad bomber, yes she had packed her own bags, yes she could show her return tickets, yes she could provide addresses where they could come get her if she was lying, no she had never been, wasn't now or was ever likely to be a member of the Communist Party, nor was she here for an immoral purpose (the last two, to be fair, were questions they never asked) … thank you, enjoy your visit and have a nice day, next please and stand behind the yellow line – and waited for a fixed-tariff cab to take her into Manhattan.

She checked into the hotel, it was everything Karen had promised, and though she was feeling a little jaded after the flight she couldn't wait to make her initial exploration of the neighbourhood. It was a hot, humid Manhattan afternoon but, hay, this was New York and it was time for that first bite at the Big Apple.

Rachel strode to the front door and caught the blast of steamy heat from the streets. She decided to make a quick square tour … first left, then walk two blocks and turn right, two more blocks and turn right and eventually she figured she would find herself back at the hotel. A little trailer for the coming attractions.

Then she would have a good sleep and awaken ready for her planned interviews. New York, New York: It's a Wonderful Town!

Rachel had once flown to London as the guest of a film distribution company to interview Keanu Reeves, who told her fame and fortune were all very well but he regretted not being able to stroll casually along a street without being mobbed.

Rachel understood this but she offered him her own theory on the subject. If, she said, he were to come to Belfast and walk along Royal Avenue hardly anybody would bother him. Not because he wasn't famous but because most people would look at him and think he just happened to look like Keanu Reeves, but since Keanu Reeves couldn't possibly be calmly walking around Belfast without the protection of muscle-bound guards he must simply be somebody who looked like Keanu Reeves.

On her return to the hotel she walked through the lobby and saw a man sitting in the corner leafing through the New York Times. She went to the elevators and recalled her theory.

Jayne conducted her own short square tour and returned to a dream-filled sleep, with her arms wrapped contentedly around a big pillow.

TWELVE

BEFORE leaving for her meeting with the Amtrak people, Jayne reminded herself of the names of the people she had arranged to see. Jayne sorted through the documents she felt she would need, plus her notebook. She grabbed a quick coffee and Danish in the hotel café and took a cab that dropped her off at the Summer Street side of South Station.

She crossed the concourse to the Club Acela Lounge on the mezzanine and told the man at the desk that she had an appointment with Mr Carl Dunning and asked where she might find him. The man took her back out to the concourse and indicated a door.

The meeting was held in an office overlooking the concourse and she could see two trains waiting at the platforms beyond. Large flasks of coffee, with Amtrak logo mugs, cream and sugar, were spaced around the table.

Introductions were made by Carl Dunning – two of the four Amtrak people had travelled up from Washington – and coffee offered and passed around.

The fact that the BBC was interested in making a documentary series on the railway system clearly impressed them, so Jayne did not mention that the proposed project was her own and still in the early stages of its uncertain life.

Marie, the perky redhead Jayne remembered talking to in Washington, was enthusiastic about the series, suggesting that Jayne should really start the coast-to-coast journey on the Downeaster from Portland since that was the real Eastern end of the routes that would end in San Diego.

Carl thought that while the California Zephyr was one of the most spectacular rides anybody could take – as she would see for herself – she might consider taking the Empire Builder along the border with Canada from Chicago through Michigan, North Dakota, Montana and Washington State to Seattle, then pick up the Coast Starlight from there down the Pacific Coast to San Fransisco and Los Angeles. The BBC crew could return to Chicago on the Zephyr and not miss going through the Rockies.

Diane, one of the local Amtrak people, asked if the series was only for radio. She thought a television series would be better. Jayne agreed, adding that it was also in the pipeline, along with a possible coffee-table book.

Ideas, suggestions and offers of assistance – even allowing for the fact that Amtrak spent a great deal of its time fending off requests for free tickets from journalists – flew back and forth across the table and Jayne scribbled them all down, growing more and more confident that she could sell the idea to her bosses.

One other thing that earned Jayne bonus points with the Amtrak people was that she, and her friend, had paid for the entire trip themselves. No freeloading there.

The meeting became a friendly chat about what Northern Ireland was like, what she and Rachel could expect on their trip and how much they were going to enjoy it.

"And one last thing," Marie said, fishing in her briefcase as proceedings drew to a close, "I checked on your tickets and saw that you and your friend – Rachel Andrews, isn't it? – had booked single Roomettes. Well, I've managed to get you together in a Bedroom on the Zephyr, it has its own toilet and shower. Sorry I couldn't manage one on the Limited, this is a busy time for us and the New York and Boston trains are all packed."

Jayne thanked her as Marie handed over the sleeper ticket for the Bedroom.

She returned to the hotel elated. It was just going on lunch-time and she anxiously wondered if Brad had called. She went to her room and saw a red light winking on her 'phone. She picked it up and was told that a Mr Brad Carey had called at 11.30 that morning. She was given a number to call back.

She took a deep breath to steady herself and dialled.

"Hello, Carey, Shulenberg Associates, how may I help you?"

Wow! Brad did not just work there, he owned it!

She asked to speak to Mr Carey, giving her name.

"Oh yes, Miss McGregor, he said to put you straight through if you called back. Just hold on."

IF she called back; as if she wouldn't.

"Hi," Brad said, "How did your Amtrak meeting go?"

She filled him in on its success.

"Interesting you got to meet Marie Gilpin, she's one of the people that colleague of mine I mentioned on the 'plane dealt with. She's the one contact you need to keep in with. If it helps I'll get John to give her a call and sing your praises."

"Everything helps, I'd appreciate that."

"So," he said, "I hope you're free for the rest of the day ... the Grand Tour is ready to hit the bricks. Are you up for it?"

She was.

"Lovely. I'll pick you up in, say, an hour's time. Wear sensible shoes, you're going to be doing a lot of walking ... and, er ..."

"... and, er ... what?"

"Look, don't think I'm being pushy, but would you like to see my little Yankee village, all those picket fences and white churches? I'd really love to show you around. No pressure, honestly, just a thought."

"And a very sweet one," Jayne said, "Of course I'd love to see it."

"Great! Why don't you check out of the hotel, can you do that, and come stay over? I'll get you back in time for the train, day after tomorrow isn't it? Can you do that?"

"Yes," Jayne laughed, "I'm already out on the pavement surrounded by my luggage. I'll take a shower, find my sensible shoes and see you in an hour."

She checked out, slightly embarrassed at having to assure the receptionist that she had absolutely no complaints about the hotel but a friend had unexpectedly arrived back in town and was picking her up. Suitably mollified the reception adjusted the charge on her MasterCard and took Jayne's luggage into safe keeping until the unexpectedly arrived friend came.

Jayne took her jacket and scurried out to wait for Brad.

"No problems about doing a quick bunk?" he asked on arrival.

"No, I just felt a little red-faced about it. Is it OK that I've left my luggage in the hotel?"

"Sure, we'll pick it up later. Now, if you'll form an orderly line we'll commence the tour. First a coffee in Faneuil Hall and a look around its many little shops, then it's off to sit in Boston Common to watch the world go past. How's that sound for starters?"

Jayne waved him forward: "Lead on, Mr Carey. I shall fall in line beside you if that's allowed."

As they walked Brad reached across to her and held her hand. She found herself tingling like a teenager on her first date.

And tour the city they did, each step of the way accompanied by a funny lesson in the history of the sights along the two-mile Freedom Trail, Beacon Hill, Paul Revere House, the Tea Party boat and, of course, Cheers.

They walked for several hours until they returned to the sea-front at the hotel and collapsed exhausted on a bench.

"That was wonderful, thank you," she said, and reached over and kissed him.

"Well, I won't bother asking for my usual tip," he said and returned the kiss.

"So where is this mysterious village of yours?" Jayne asked, "I hope it's not called Amityville."

"Certainly not," he protested, "It's an hour up the coast, just north of a town called Lynn. It's called East Bayport, which has always amused the citizens since there has never been a North, South or West Bayport. Not even a plain old Bayport. If you sneeze or blink you'll be through it before you realise … one main street, that's Main Street, and several side streets – First, Second, Third, Fourth and Revolution Streets – running off it. Through the village, turn right at the white-painted church and you're at Massachusetts Bay."

They collected Jayne's luggage and he carried it back to a near-by car park where he loaded it into a Jeep.

"You like classical music?" he asked when they got out of downtown Boston.

Jayne nodded and he punched on the radio.

"Tell me about Carey Towers," she said, "And don't leave anything out ... like you did about actually owning your own Boston Legal law firm. And, by the way, don't think for one minute I believe you about Agatha Whatshername being a 60-year-old granny."

"She is, I may even have a photograph of her at home to prove it. And I'm just one of several owners, I just didn't want to sound conceited."

"So," Jayne repeated, "Carey Towers."

"Doesn't quite make it as high as a tower," he began, "It's an early 19th Century whaling captain's house – he no longer lives there, by the way – two storeys, plus a cobwebby attic in well weathered timber, which I have painted white … painted very badly.

"Four bedrooms, three bathrooms with showers that seem to work only on alternate days, a large lounge with a stone fireplace a small family could live in, a dining room, a conservatory, a kitchen that's a ghastly mixture of traditional and modern and there's a veranda that runs right around the house. It's all very New England, if you see what I mean. It's been in the Carey family for years and years.

"Let me see now if I've got it all … oh yes, it sits back from the road with a garden front and back, and a stone-slabbed path leading down to the sea. There's a really good beach, actually, good for long, thoughtful walks.

"And, last but by no means least, there's Barney …"

Ah, now the full family background, Jayne thought.

"Your son …"

Brad laughed: "Not bad going. It's taken you until now to wonder if I'm really a married man cheating on his betrayed wife and family. So before you say anything else, I'm not married and Barney is my Red Setter – Irish, too – and he thinks he's the real owner of Carey Towers.

"I came close once. I was engaged to a girl, but she was killed in an auto accident. It was a really awful night and she was driving to Gloucester when a truck skidded across the road and took her out. After that I didn't want to know about love or romance, I just got on with my career."

He glanced across at her and winked: "Tit for tat … I assume you aren't married."

"No, I'm an old spinster of the parish. I pretend it's because I'm a career girl on the fast track."

"Good," Brad said, "then this, as Mr Bogard famously observed, could be the start of a beautiful friendship."

"We'll see, won't we?" Jayne said, giving him a gentle nudge in the ribs, "Anyway, we'll always have East Bayport."

They reached East Bayport, indicated by a sign that read: Welcome to EAST BAYPORT. Pop: 7,352.

The '2' had been chalked out and '4' was written beside it.

"See the twins have arrived," Brad said, "We're Yankees in these parts, we like things to be absolutely correct."

He pulled into the side of the road and drew her to him. They

109

kissed.

"Welcome to East Bayport. I'm delighted you decided to come."

Jayne held his face in her hands and looked into his eyes. She was delighted she had decided to come. She kissed him.

He pulled back onto the road and drove slowly along Main Street, pointing out the various quaint little shops and what families lived in the houses.

"It's beautiful," Jayne said as the arts and craft shops, the antique shops, the boutiques, a fish tackle shop, a coffee house-cum-bookstore, a red-brick school, the required auto repair shop-filling station and the pastel-painted timber houses with their neat, flower-filled lawns and hanging baskets and picket fences glided past.

"The legend is that East Bayport doesn't really exist. Stephen King would love it. They say it appears out of nowhere before anybody's up and disappears after everyone's gone to bed, very spooky. They even say the Mayor is really Walt Disney," Brad said, and Jayne laughed and gave him a playful punch.

They drove up to the church – with Brad honking the horn and waving to people on the street – and stopped. He took her hand and led her to the stone wall around the old graveyard surrounding the church.

"This is the church of Saint John the Divine, very Presbyterian. Back in the early days of the community – in the 1700s – the first minister was called, I kid you not, Recompense Slingsberry. Nobody could possibly live up to that moniker so today the minister is plain William Jones, more in keeping with our New England mentality."

He took her to the side of the church and pointed down Revolution Street.

"See that building on the left, that's Charlie's Clam Shack ... that's where I'm going to treat you to the most delicious Seafood Crespelle you'll ever taste. Think you could tackle that?"

"Yes, I'm famished," Jayne said.

They returned to the Jeep and Brad drove down a dusty road towards the sea, glistening and foaming ahead of them.

They came to the house and got out.

"I'll come back for the luggage, let me show you around," Brad said, taking her hand and leading her through the front gate.

A shingle sign just inside a rope fence read Schooner Cove and the pink pebble path wound past islands of bobbing flowers. A brass ship's bell hung beside the front door.

"Ring the bell and prepare yourself," Brad said.

Jayne swung the rope and the bell tanged several times. An excited Setter raced around the house, barking and bouncing around Brad: "This is Barney … Barney meet Miss Jayne McGregor. She's Irish, like you."

Jayne stooped to ruffle Barney's long, flopping ears and he ran around her in thrilled circles.

"Well I guess you can come in, Barney's fallen in love with you," Brad said, exchanging a quick glance with her.

Inside, the house was cool and welcoming. Cream walls and dark low beams, in the lounge two deep blue sofas and two matching chairs were grouped in front of the log-filled fireplace. The walls were covered with prints of sailing ships and seascape paintings and one wall had a floor to ceiling bookcase. At the window overlooking the sea there was an old mounted telescope. Richly-coloured woollen rugs were scattered around the knotted plank floor.

He gave her a quick tour of the house, accompanied by Barney who raced ahead from room to room and raced back for more ear ruffling.

Upstairs he took her to a large bedroom with a glorious view of the beach and the rolling waves. It had a large, four-poster bed covered with a brightly-coloured American patchwork quilt. A dressing-table sat against the wall at the end of the bed and a small, round table with wicker chairs was at the window that opened onto a balcony.

"The bathroom is over there," Brad indicated a dark pine door, "I think it's the turn of this shower to work. Do you like it?"

"Oh Brad," she said, "I love it, it's absolutely perfect."

"OK, so you make yourself at home and I'll go fetch your luggage. I'll bring you lots of towels and make us a pot of coffee. I've booked a table at Charlie's for 7.45pm so you have plenty of time to relax and explore the old pile."

As he turned to leave, Jayne reached out and gently pulled him back. She put her arms around him and kissed him.

She opened the bedroom window and leaned on the iron railing of the balcony, looking out over the lawn to the sand dunes, the wide golden beach and the sea. The early evening air was filled with the salty tang carried on a light breeze.

She wandered from bedroom to bedroom, accompanied by Barney – Brad's, she guessed, was the one at the front of the house since it had an antique roll-top desk against the window and a computer on a desk beside it. Files and papers were stacked neatly on shelves.

Downstairs she poked her head into the kitchen and watched him getting the coffee ready.

In the lounge she looked at the silver-framed photographs dotted around the room. She picked up one of Brad standing beside a beautiful, dark-haired woman. They were posing on what looked like a wooden jetty with a boat moored behind them.

"That's Stella, my sister. She lives just along the coast, a couple of miles away," Brad said, carrying a tray with the coffee mugs into the room, "You'll meet her tomorrow. She and her husband, Tony, make furniture," he looked around, "some of their pieces are here … that chair, and that table."

He set the tray on the table and handed her one of the mugs. He scanned the photographs until he found what he was looking for. He handed it to her.

"And the lady in the middle of this group is the famous Mrs Agatha Pinkerton … so you see, she's nothing like you'd find on Boston Legal. She's the best secretary in the world, in all honesty she actually runs the company. That was taken at one of our regular company clambakes … we're very much into bonding."

They sat on the sofa and Brad filled in some more of the Carey history: how his great-great grandfather had come to what was then merely a cluster of houses and started a small whaling fleet, how his grandfather had married a local beauty and built the house, how his father chose not to become a whaler but a lawyer and passed that new tradition to Brad.

"But I still retain the family's love of the sea, even if it's just pottering about in the Bay and calling into the small villages along the coast. The boat in the photograph is mine … I don't get to use it as often as I'd like. You know what they say about being a boat owner: it's like digging a big hole and throwing hundred Dollar bills into it every other hour."

"And you live here all on your own?"

"Yes, I think I'm fast becoming the village recluse. Well, it's not quite as bad as that. I get a lot of friends calling in for week-ends and I'm on the boards of a couple of local arts organisations and charities, so a lot of the meetings are held here. The company clambakes are held here. We do a terrific annual Bayport Drama Festival every

May, nothing too spectacular mind you, but lots of the surrounding towns and villages have amateur drama groups and they all gather for the do. Great fun."

He checked his watch: "I'm running out of supplies, so why don't you hang out, get ready for Charlie's and I'll go get some food."

Jayne treated herself to a hot, refreshing shower – it was the shower's turn to work – and opened her case to see what she could wear. She found the dress she had packed for any possible special occasions – and tonight, she decided, was a very special occasion – and laid it out across the bed.

She dried her long, dark hair with a big fluffy towel and fingered it into a sexy windblown style, adding a thin strand of blue ribbon. She slipped into the silkiest underwear she had and put on the ankle-length blue silk dress with sandals.

Brad knocked gently at her door and asked if she was decent. She was, she said, thinking to herself that her thoughts were anything but. She opened the door.

He looked at her and smiled: "Charlie's will never be the same again … you're beautiful."

They walked down to the lounge and out to the veranda at the rear of the house. Brad excused himself and returned presently to drape a delicately-woven antique white lace shawl around her shoulders.

They stood with his arms around her waist. Jayne reached down and squeezed his hands tightly against her. Her head was tilted back to rest on his chest.

Delta confirmed the travel arrangements of Jackson and Wendy: Tuesday, the company Lear to Chicago; Wednesday, Thursday and Friday screwing their brains out in a fancy hotel. She called Collins and relayed the details. Collins jotted the details down and called his contact, the sort of contact who went by the sole name of Cross … the contact merely grunted and rang off.

THIRTEEN

RACHEL slept soundly and awoke at 10am. She stretched out in the luxury of her comfortable bed, sunshine streaming through the window, and ran the day's coming schedule through her head: she had a meeting with the Cookstown PR lady on Madison Avenue at 11.30am – give that an hour, she figured – and an afternoon chat with the chef from Larne, when the lunch-time rush had passed. Pick up a couple of magazines and see if there were any useful leads she could follow up. Hit the shops, of course.

Deliciously, the rest of the day she had set aside for some serious sightseeing and even more serious shopping. She mentally hugged herself … she was in New York, wow! Look out New York!

She got ready, wondering how dear Jayne was doing, all alone and up to her ears in boring meetings in buttoned-down Boston. She dressed in a light linen suit and white T-shirt, checked her notebook and pens – and travellers' cheques – into her bag and rode the elevator downstairs for a quick coffee: no power breakfast for a busy, story-seeking journo. And dedicated shopper.

Marvin watched from across the street as she came out of the hotel and stood holding up her hand until a cab pulled up and she got in. He flagged down a following cab and with no hint of melodrama told the driver to "follow that cab." The driver shrugged, it had been done before and with more style.

He trailed Rachel's cab along Madison Avenue, wondering how he was going to get at her. Her cab swerved into the pavement, double-parked amid an outburst of angry honking and bad language. She hopped out and ran into a building.

"Stop here," Marvin said, pushing a $20 through the grill behind the driver's head. He crossed the road, jumping and side-stepping between the traffic, and looked down the copper notice-board in the building's lobby.

It told him nothing except that every business indicated seemed to be a marketing, public relations or advertising outfit, with a couple of accountants and a theatrical agency thrown in.

She could be in any one of over 100 offices in the 16-storey building. He looked around the lobby, past the bank of pinging elevators and saw a coffee shop. He stopped at the small newspaper and cigar kiosk and bought a Times before continuing to the café. He bought a coffee and a buttered muffin and took them to a table at the window, from where he could look back along the corridor.

He opened the 'paper and watched the bustling women primp past in their power dresses.

He waited for just past an hour, wondering if she had left by another door, and then he saw her emerge from an elevator with another woman. Together they walked, deep in conversation, to the front door and into the street where they shook hands, exchanged cards – how very American – and went their separate ways. He left the 'paper and his untouched seventh cup of coffee and walked quickly to the door, joining the throng of people on the street.

He saw her, several yards ahead, and fell back to keep her in his sights.

Rachel was the typical tourist, craning her neck at the towering skyscrapers, nearly getting mashed at the street corners because she hadn't yet worked out that traffic turning a certain way has the right of way, collecting dirty looks because the warning 'DON'T WALK' means just that. Stupid little bitch, he thought, you don't walk aimlessly along a Manhattan street like you've never fucking set eyes on a tall building before. Doing that you might as well carry a banner telling people that you're a moronic out-of-towner and you're just there to be dragged up an alley and mugged.

You don't progress down a Manhattan street window by window. Rachel did this so often that he was forever forced to slide into convenient doorways. He looked stupid, and if he didn't strike people as downright suspicious something was wrong.

Finally he realised that he wasn't going to grab her out in the open anyway. Even your average, couldn't-give-a-toss New Yorker would figure he was up to no good. He watched her and let her go.

He made his way back to the hotel and thought about what he would do now. He sat in the lobby and thought it through.

He went to the reception desk and asked the girl if he could borrow a pen and a piece of paper so he could leave an important message for one the guests. He gave her his best smile and it seemed to work. She beamed her perfect teeth and glistening red lips at him, reached under the counter and put a sheet of headed notepaper and pen on top, with a white envelope.

He scribbled some gibberish, put the paper into the envelope and sealed it. He wrote Rachel's name on the envelope and watched as the receptionist turned and pushed it into a box with a key dangling above it from a hook: Room 241. Thank you very much.

He walked to the elevator and got out at Rachel's floor.

The corridor was empty except for a cleaning trolley standing outside an open room. Inside he could hear a woman singing as she pushed a cleaner over the carpet. He walked past and found 241. He waited until the maid came out of the room and pushed a bundle of dirty sheets into a plastic bag at the bottom of the trolley and lifted a fresh set off the top.

He walked back to her: "Excuse me, I'm in Room 241. I've left my keys inside and I'm in a hurry, could you let me in?"

The maid gave him her happens-all-the-time smile and fished in her white coat for a bunch of keys. He followed her to the door and when she had opened it he gave her a $20 bill. She smiled and resumed her song as she went back to making the room ready for the next visitor.

Inside he looked around. The maid had not reached Rachel's room yet for the bed was unmade and clothes were thrown untidily over a chair. She had not yet unpacked for a case lay open at the foot of the bed, its contents hardly disturbed.

He began sifting carefully through the case, feeling around the inside. He found nothing and sat on the bed looking around. He saw the silver metal laptop case under the writing desk at the window and got up. He thumbed the locks and the lid opened. He lifted the computer out and saw the envelope underneath. He opened it. It contained her airline tickets and a folder with the Amtrak logo on the top right-hand corner.

He pulled the documents out. She was booked on the Thursday Lake Shore Limited to Chicago and on the following day's California Zephyr to San Fransisco. Other tickets covered later journeys on the Coast Starlight from Oakland to Los Angeles and Pacific Surfliner from LA to San Diego and back to LA.

He took a pen and slip of notepaper from the desk drawer and

117

wrote down the trains, the departure times and the sleepers she had booked. Now he was getting somewhere. It would, if need be, be part of his Plan B, though he had not abandoned the idea of getting Rachel during her remaining time in New York.

He replaced the laptop and slipped it back under the desk, wiping the case with a tissue, and smoothed out the clothes in the case, also wiping it with the tissue.

He wiped the door handle and still holding the tissue opened it and stepped into the corridor. The maid was spraying the room with squirts of freshener as he walked quietly to the elevators.

He returned to his apartment to freshen up and change his shirt, vowing to return to his watch on the hotel later in the evening. She might go out for a stroll, to see the bright lights of Broadway, and if she did he might have a chance. More and more he grew convinced that she knew about the missing money, might even be spending some of it on this trip.

It was 6:30 by the time he resumed his position across from the hotel. He sat on a bench pretending to read a book but really watching every movement in and out of the building. It was a balmy evening, warm and humid from the heat of the July day. A breeze rustled through the leaves as he listened to the throb of the traffic from the nearby avenues and streets. Manhattan was swinging into its on-the-town stride, the restaurants and theatres and galleries working themselves into a frenzy for the coming entertainment. There was a palpable heartbeat to the city, it was as alive – more so, even – an entity as any of the people he watched walking along the street.

He watched as a cab drew up outside the hotel and a woman got out, stooped to speak to the driver and entered the lobby. The cab remained, its engine ticking and burbing over, and the woman came from the hotel accompanied by Rachel. They got in and the cab moved off.

Marvin pulled out his cell 'phone and called the hotel, asking if he could speak to Rachel Andrews in Room 241. He listened to the receptionist conduct a smothered conversation and then she came back on.

"I'm sorry, Miss Andrews just left for the evening. I think she's gone to one of the theatres with a friend. I don't know which theatre it is. May I leave a message?"

He rang off. He thought for a moment and suddenly recognised the woman, she was the one he had seen Rachel with that morning in the Madison Avenue building.

"Shit!" he said, startling an elderly blue-rinse walking her yappy little dot of a dog. The dog jumped away from his bench barking furiously and the old cow glared at him before moving on. He mouthed a sullen 'fuck off.'

He returned to Murray Hill. Tomorrow, Rachel, is another day.

It had been an unexpected bonus of an evening out for Rachel, the best seats at a full-blown, smash-hit Broadway musical, courtesy of her Cookstown hostess who had handled all the publicity for the production, and a visit backstage for a little extra surprise the Cookstown hostess had been holding in reserve ... one of the minor stars was a young actress from Newry for whom much was expected. An exclusive interview and several colour pics already on their way to the News Letter, plus a great meal in a swish theatrical restaurant with several members of the cast, rounded off a perfect day that saw the young reporter deposited back at the hotel just after midnight, exhausted and happy.

The following day – check: later the same day – she had arranged to meet a genuine Belfast-born NYPD cop, their rendezvous set for outside the Lincoln Center – must remember that, er not re, Americans don't know how to spell - under the Mostly Mozart banner at the fountains, at noon.

That would give her time for a long lie-in, a leisurely visit to a nearby deli to sample a typical Manhattan breakfast and to return to her room to compose and send over the interviews and work on the first of her Andrews in America travel pieces ... she wondered if the News Letter might consider setting up a New York Bureau, with her in charge, of course. As Shopping Correspondent.

Lincoln Centre – er - for the Performing Arts – ER, remember it's ER – was started in 1959 and is the cultural heart of the city, just across from Central Park. The square, glass-fronted building with its tall, arched pillars, occupies over 16 acres and within its walls are a dozen of the world's most famous artistic organisations, ranging from the Julliard School, the Metropolitan Opera, the New York City Ballet, the New York Philharmonic, the New York City Opera to the New York Public Library for the Performing Arts, as well as drama, dance and music schools and shops and restaurants.

Rachel stood on the pavement at the bottom of the steps and gazed at the unforgettable building.

She walked up the steps and spotted her subject standing beneath the fluttering Mozart banner. He was pointing directions to a group of camera-laden tourists.

"You must be Danny McCarroll," Rachel said when the tourists had moved off.

"And with that Norn Iron accent you must be Rachel," the NYPD officer said, holding out his hand.

"Good to hear you haven't lost yours," she said, shaking his hand.

He asked if she'd like a quick tour of the Center and together they walked across the paved forecourt and into the building.

"This is part of my beat," he explained, "so I know most of the people here. We can stop off for a coffee afterwards and you can do your interview, though I'm not sure what you want."

"Oh, don't worry," she said, "nothing to worry you. I don't know if your media people explained, but I'm a reporter on the News Letter and I'm just doing stuff on people from back home who are now living and working in the States. It won't be too painful, I promise you."

He laughed: "That's OK then. Just a word of warning, though: it's not quite like a Hollywood movie or Law and Order."

"Good," she said, "I just want the life and times of Danny McCarroll, one of Ireland's finest on the mean streets of NYC."

"Yes, I can see now that you're a newspaper reporter."

He was, she noted, a good looking cop, impressive in his blue uniform and not, as quite a lot of the policemen she had seen seemed to be, alarmingly overweight. The media people had promised to wire a photograph of him to Belfast.

After the tour, seated in one of the Center's cafes, he told her his story.

He was from the Ardoyne in Belfast and had always wanted to be either a policeman or to join the army – "But," he added, "it wouldn't have been the smartest of moves joining the RUC or one of the Queen's regiments while living in Ardoyne." – so 10 years ago he came to New York with a Gaelic team, loved it and stayed. He picked up jobs as a barman and in the building trade, studied hard, got through the Academy and had been a cop for eight years.

He was married to an Italian girl, had a young son and worked along Broadway, the south side of Central Park and, of course, the Lincoln. For good measure he threw in several stories about the characters he came across on his beat and about some of the scrapes he'd been involved in.

He also recalled a couple of colourful stories about the many police dramas filmed in New York: "It can be strange watching Brad Pitt and Leonardo Di Caprio pretending to be me, sort of thing."

Rachel wrote furiously, it would make a terrific piece. Back on the forecourt she asked a passing tourist to take a photograph of her and Danny on her camera.

"What are you doing today, then?" Danny asked.

"This is my last full day in New York," she explained, "I'm off to Chicago tomorrow. So today I'm going to hit the town and see as much of it as I can, all the usual touristy things: the Empire State, the Flat Iron, the Statue of Liberty, a walk around the Park, sneak a look inside the Plaza, see Trump Tower, maybe take a ride on the Staten Island Ferry, take in the United Nations, wander around SoHo ..."

"Wow!" he said, holding up his hands, "Take it easy, lady ... you'll be whacked if you try a schedule like that. Why not take one of the boat trips around Manhattan, that way you'll see a lot more, like the Mayor's house at Gracey Mansion and the Cloisters. If you still have enough energy left you really should pay the Metropolitan Museum of Art a visit.

"If you're anything like Maria, my missus, that'll keep you out of the shops."

They parted with a hug and Rachel watched as he walked off to look after several more lost tourists.

Marvin had tracked her from the hotel and was thrown off guard when he saw her with the cop. Had she sussed him out? Had she recognised him?

He was getting really seriously pissed off stalking her through the streets, knowing that it would be impossible to snatch her. He was getting really seriously pissed off, and when he was pissed off ...!

Furious over the time he had wasted he waved down a cab and returned to his apartment ... time for Plan B.

He logged into the Amtrak site and checked the departure time of the Lake Shore Limited. The train left Penn at 3.20pm, he would make his move then. He scrolled down the time-table and worked out that he could grab her and, maybe, get her off without anybody noticing somewhere along the route, at Poughkeepsie or Hudson or Croton-Harmon, say.

He flicked over to the on-line booking page and bought a reserved coach seat to Albany-Rensselaer. It was a strong option. He was done with getting pissed off.

FOURTEEN

CHARLIE'S Clam Shack turned out to be just that, a medium-sized weathered wooden shack standing, somehow, at the far end of Revolution Street. Across the street the sea churned and sizzled over the sandy beach. There was a gravel car park in front, packed with vehicles, and there were several tables laid out along the front veranda.

From a tilting, Z-shaped tin chimney curled a whisp of white smoke, taken by the light breeze into a copse of trees at the rear of the building.

When Brad had found a space in the car park and helped Jayne from the Jeep a forest of hands rose in greeting like a Mexican Wave as the diners recognised him. He placed his hand gently around Jayne's waist and steered her towards the smiling spectators.

He took her along the row of tables and introduced her: a sea of friendly faces and a litany of names she knew she would never remember.

As he opened the door into the shack he whispered in Jayne's ear: "You gathered a lot of fans out there. You certainly boosted my standing in the community. I think I'll kidnap you, East Bayport needs you more than the Lake Shore Limited."

Jayne dimpled and blushed, feeling all their eyes on her.

Charlie saw them as soon as they entered, scurrying around the tables – all 12 of them, Jayne counted, and all but one occupied – to throw himself on Brad.

Charlie was a small, tubby, red-faced man with a great, welcoming smile. He wore a chef's hat at a regular jaunty angle and around his waist was tied a red-squared apron.

He untangled himself from Brad and looked set to engulf Jayne with the same bear-hug until Brad waved a finger at him and said:

"Let the lady eat first and if you don't poison her she might award you with a small peck on the cheek."

Charlie pretended disappointment: "Poison her, she will think she has visited heaven when she tastes what I've prepared for her."

Brad introduced him to Jayne and Charlie ushered them through the restaurant – again a slow procession of table-hopping and introductions – to a table set apart from the others.

Though it was still light, the sun dipping towards the sea, two fat red candles spluttered and danced in the middle of the table, their light sparkling off the plates and glasses and silver laid out on a sea-blue tablecloth.

Charlie beat Brad in the race to pull out the seat for Jayne. He winked as she and Brad settled in: "She is beautiful … no, what a paltry word that is," he turned his smile on Jayne, "Magnificent!"

Jayne hoped her flushed cheeks did not outdo the candles.

"It's OK," Brad said, "Just nibble your nails while Charlie finishes, it might be the only meal you get tonight."

But, of course, it wasn't. The meal was, well, beautiful and magnificent and what paltry words they were to describe it. The accompanying wine – the bottles still with a hint of dust on them to announce their vintage – was equally beautiful and magnificent.

They lingered and talked and laughed … and held hands across the table and Jayne wondered what on earth was happening to her. On their way out she rewarded a beaming Charlie.

"If you must leave us," he said, "you must promise to return as quickly as you can … my humble restaurant will now be a much duller place."

They drove back to the house and Brad took her hand and led her along the path to the beach. The sun had been edged from a star-speckled sky by a big yellow moon that admired its reflection in the rolling waves.

Jayne took off her sandals and squished her toes in the sand as they walked at the water's edge. The beach was deserted; it was a lyrical night.

They sat on a dune and Brad turned her face to his. They kissed and Jayne lay back on the soft sand as he slowly undressed her. She reached up and drew him down to her and into her.

He lifted her, still naked, and carried her back to the house. They lay entwined on her four-poster and made love again. He looked at her, tracing his fingers softly around her breasts and down her stomach, kissing each caress until she moaned softly and arched her back. She fell into a deep and utterly happy sleep.

The sun was up and well into its day's chores when he kissed her awake and put a tray of juice, coffee and a hot buttered muffin on the bed beside her. He was wearing a white fluffy dressing gown, tied loosely at the waist. Jayne stirred at the smell of the coffee and smiled.

She sipped at the cold juice and reached across the tray. She tugged at the dressing gown belt and took him in her hand.

"Where am I, what's your name again?" she said with a smile.

"OK, Miss McGregor, time to get up ..."

"I see you beat me to it, Mr Carey ..."

"Behave, this is New England; whatever would the neighbours say? Finish your breakfast – it's almost brunch – take a shower and we'll go exploring."

She stretched like a contented cat.

"Those lovely legs have given me an idea," Brad said.

"I thought you wanted me to behave?"

"I do, for the moment anyway. Like I said, those legs have given me an idea ... we're going to explore on bikes. I have a couple of old bone-shakers somewhere. We need the exercise."

"Didn't we get enough last night ... the bone-shaking and the exercise?"

He stood up: "I'm off for a shower. You have half-an-hour to get ready."

He was waiting for her at the front door, standing between two cycles. She wore a pink denim shirt and a pair of white tennis shorts. She had put on a bikini and a pair of trainers. He took the rolled towel from her – holding up the one he had brought – and put it into the saddle-bag.

She twirled and asked: "How do I look, is this suitable attire for buttoned-down Bayport?"

"Just as long as the Rev Recompense Slingsberry doesn't see you, he'll have you burned as a beguiling witch. Hop on, I assume you can wobble about on this machine."

"Just watch me, buster ... and try to keep up."

They raced along the path and turned towards the town.

They left the cycles at the filling station and made their way, shop by shop, along Main Street. He pointed out pieces of furniture and old prints in the antique shop window and added some historical background, they wandered around the arts and craft shop where he bought her a dumpy, wide-eyed red whale wearing a knitted hat that read FROM EAST BAYPORT: WHALE MEET AGAIN! They giggled at the lovely awfulness of it.

In the café-bookstore they had a coffee and Jayne bought a thin volume on the history of East Bayport. They looked at the brightly-feathered flies in the fishing tackle shop and retraced their way back to the cycles.

"I called my sister and, naturally, she's desperate to meet you. Are you up to it?" he asked anxiously.

"Of course I am," Jayne said, "I promise to behave myself … always mindful of your standing in the community. OK, let's go. Will your creaking knees make it?"

"Just follow me."

They mounted and took off along what was left of Main Street, past the church, past the house and onto a narrow, black-top road that skirted the beach.

"You have a nice butt, Mr Carey!" Jayne called to him.

The morning after meeting Officer McCarroll and taking the boat ride around Manhattan, Rachel sat at the writing desk in her hotel room and wrote up the interview and the opening travel piece. When she had sent them to the News Letter she checked them off on a list she had started in her notebook: NYC: Interviews with Manhattan PR, chef, actress, NYPD cop, travel feature.

She hadn't done badly for just a couple of days in the city, certainly she had sent enough to buy herself plenty of time before she had to start looking for fresh material.

She was looking forward to meeting up with Jayne again in Albany … whatever had her friend managed to find to do in Boston?

Rachel packed her bag and tidied up the room. She took her Amtrak ticket and passport from the laptop case and put them into the inside pocket of her jacket. She almost forgot the pile of post cards she had bought for her father and Karen, Sandi and the gang at the newspaper. She would ask the receptionist to have them posted when she settled her bill. One last check of the room, nothing overlooked, nothing still left unpacked.

She paid the bill and walked out to find a cab. It was 10am, plenty of time to get to Penn Station and find the Amtrak desk.

Stella heard them arriving and ran from the cement-block building at the side of another East Bayport timber-framed house. Tony came to the door of the building and stood smiling and wiping his hands on a cloth as Brad and Jayne swished to a halt on the pebble driveway.

Brad's sister hugged him and then hugged Jayne after Brad had introduced her. Brad waved at Tony and walked over to the building. As he approached he could smell the paint and varnish and glue they used in the making of their furniture. They shook hands and went in.

"I'm so glad you could come visit," Stella said, directing Jayne to the house, "Come on, I have a nice pot of tea just brewed. We can take some into the men."

Stella was older than Brad, by just a few years, Jayne reckoned, and she was tall, slim, dark and beautiful in a country-living sort of way. Her hands were splashed with light brown varnish and small slivers of wood were caught in her hair. She noticed Jayne looking and ran her fingers through her hair, flicking the wood out.

"Sorry, gets a tad messy in there," she said, adding in case Jayne did not already know, "Tony, that's my husband, and I make furniture out in the workshop. We do quite well out of it, Tony's a brilliant carpenter," she added with pride.

She poured the tea into four delicate, special-occasions cups and opened a tin of cookies that she piled onto each plate.

"Could you bring the milk and sugar," she nodded towards a cupboard, "and come with me."

Jayne saw the sign above the door, The Bayport Collection, as she followed Stella inside.

Tony showed her around the lathes and benches, filled with pieces still under construction, and into a small showroom at the rear of the building. It was filled with beautifully-crafted tables, chairs, dressers, wardrobes, coat-stands, garden benches and even a wall of carved and polished mirrors.

"We're branching out," he told them, "Got a store up in Portland interested in these ..."

He opened a door into a smaller back room. Lined along the shelves were brightly-painted wooden toys: small cars, an old-fashioned tram-car, fire engines, a high-stacked railway engine, a big rocking horse, and a wonderful period dolls house with the front open to reveal small, dainty furniture.

"Oh," Jayne said, "how beautiful."

Stella and Tony stood with their arms around one another, smiling.

She shooed them all back to the house and through to the back patio. They sat around a long wooden table and finished their tea and cookies. Brad filled them in on his visit to Ireland, Tony brought him up to date on the latest doings in Bayport, Jayne told them about her work at the BBC, what Belfast was now like, and about her trip around the USA.

"Tony here has been to a lot of the places you intend to visit," Brad said, "He used to be a pilot with United."

"Yes," Tony said, like he was remembering another life, "Then one day I was bouncing through a snowstorm into Fargo and thought, I don't need to be doing this. Stella was sitting at home, I was missing her ... and Fargo I didn't need. I jacked it in and started the business ... never been happier."

They sat a while longer then Tony got up: "Hate to do it, but I've a customer in Boston waiting for a table and six chairs. Will you be staying?"

"No, Jayne has to get ready for Boston," Brad said, "Just called in to see the family. I can give a hand for a spell, though, if you like."

The men walked around to the side of the house ... time, Jayne figured, for Stella to do some finding out.

"Sit and I'll get us a couple of cold beers," Stella said, returning with two foaming tumblers.

And she did some finding out. More importantly she also gave Jayne some finding out about Brad: about his tragic engagement, about throwing himself into building up his law firm.

When she had finished she smiled at Jayne: "I know you two just met but I'll tell you this: I've not seen Brad look so chirpy in years. All he seems to have done the past couple of years has been work and work and work.

"I don't know where you and he will get to, early days I know, but I'll say one thing: you look like you'd be good for him, and he'd been good for you," she thought for a moment then slapped her hands on the table, "So, I'm just a nosey sister, but there you go. I hope we see you again, Jayne."

As they rode back to the house Jayne pulled alongside him and said: "They're a great couple ... but what was that about me having to get ready for Boston, unless you've decided to throw me out I don't have to catch the train until tomorrow?"

Brad winked: "Oh, I just thought we could find something to help pass an evening back at the old homestead."

"OK," Jayne said, "But we'll have to stop in town, find a food store ... tonight I'm going to cook you a meal."

"Well, lady, you cook as well?"

"Sure do. Hay, I'm an old Irish spinster who has to look after herself. Nothing for Charlie to worry about, mind you ... but something you'll enjoy, followed if you're lucky by something else you might just enjoy."

"There goes my standing ..."

They bought the food and several bottles of wine and raced back to the house. After the meal they sat on the veranda and watched another glorious sunset. When an unusual chill drifted in off the sea they went back to the lounge and Brad lit the log fire, more for effect than for heat. While he was doing this Jayne went around the room and lit the candles, forming islands of shimmering light.

She stretched out on the sofa, her head resting on his lap, his hand on her breast. Barney was snoring and snortling contentedly in front of the fire, and Jayne could not think of a nicer two days than those she had had with Brad.

Early the following morning they returned to Boston, a sudden air of uncertainty surrounding them in the Jeep. It had been an idyllic break, but Jayne's mind raced with confused, emotional thoughts of what would now become of their meeting, if anything other than the conclusion of a brief encounter. She steeled herself to the prospect that it had been nothing more than that. She felt awful.

Brad had an important meeting at 10.30 that morning and she had assured him that she did not mind waiting on her own until the train departed at noon. She would grab a handful of magazines and relax in the Acela Lounge, perhaps manage a quick walk to the shops around South Station.

They arrived at the station, found a parking spot and he carried her luggage through the restored old station to the Lounge. She gave the man – who recognised her from her earlier visit – her ticket and took a seat at the back of the Lounge. Brad brought her a newspaper and coffee and sat beside her.

They drank in unsettling silence and then he took her hand.

"I've enjoyed being with you," he began awkwardly, "I hope you did too ..."

"But ..." she said, turning to face him.

"No buts," he said, "Meeting you on the 'plane was the best thing that's happened to me in years, and taking you to Bayport ... everything was, well, everything was just perfect."

He drew her into his embrace and they kissed.

"I think I've fall ..." he began.

Jayne stopped him, a finger on his lips: "Don't say it, not yet. Stella said it was early days between us, and she was right. We have no idea if we will ever have any more days ..."

"But we'll always have East Bayport, eh?"

She managed a smile: "Yes ..."

He stood up and pulled her after him, putting his arms around her: "I'm going to miss you. And I'm going to be doing a lot more business for my clients in Ireland."

They clung to each other and finally he broke the spell. He kissed her one more time and turned to leave.

Jayne caught his hand and turned him around: "I think I've fall, as well. I'll 'phone you every day from Boston to San Diego, so have Agatha standing by."

She watched him leave the Acela and sat down with a wide, happy smile. My goodness, she thought, my bloody goodness!

Rachel found the Amtrak desk in the depths of the vast, busy Penn Station, checked in and left her luggage in the Acela Lounge. She had three hours to kill, time to explore what seemed to her to be more of a small town than a mere railway station.

She wandered around the shops, bought several magazines, a paperback copy of John Pitt's USA by RAIL – lots of useful information about the route - and a coffee to go. She took the coffee to the forecourt, found an empty bench and sat to watch the people rushing past.

Opposite her sat a young woman surrounded by carrier bags. She was dressed as though she had just travelled from the 1960s through a time-warp. She was reading a paperback and Rachel squinted to see its title: The Secrets of the Crystal: Changing Your Life.

The young woman and the paperback seemed, to Rachel, to be in perfect harmony.

Marvin, still seriously pissed off at his fruitless chase of Rachel around Manhattan, prepared to leave his apartment for Penn Station. Not that any of his recent plans had gone the way he would have wanted, but he intended to finally grab her, get her off the train and get the information about the missing money he was now convinced she had.

He checked his watch – it was 2.15 – and headed for the door … just as his 'phone started ringing. He swore, debated whether to just leave and let it ring or answer it and walked back to pick up the receiver.

"Shit!" he muttered to himself as he heard the voice of the man he had met at the Empire State.

"My associates have asked me to call you, Marvin," the man said and Marvin listened to the cold, over-calm voice, "They're a bit worried that your efforts to resolve the problem of the newspaper reporter have not been successful … you understand that they don't like to be worried."

"Yes, I understand fully," Marvin said, "I have the matter well in hand. Of course, you understand, how difficult it is to grab somebody on a busy New York street …" like fuck his caller knew, stuffed shirt pretending to be tough, just try it yourself you fuck, "I've got the matter well in hand …"

He flicked back the sleeve of his jacket, the minute hand seemed to have speeded up.

"In fact," his caller said, "my associates are not fully convinced this, what's her name …"

"Andrews, Rachel Andrews," Marvin spat out the name, get a fucking move on, he was running out of time.

"Yes, Rachel Andrews. My associates are not convinced she does actually know anything about the money."

"She knows," Marvin said, "She knows and I intend to find out everything she knows. Tell your associates everything is under control."

"However …"

Shit! Shit! Shit! This he didn't need … a lecture like he was a small boy caught playing with himself in the garden shed.

"However, they are wondering if any further move against her would be worth the risk."

"She knows, she knows about the money," Marvin had to stop himself shouting now, "I'm certain she knows. All I can tell you, again, is to leave it with me. Have I ever let you down in the past … Harling himself, that family in Houston, the trouble in Detroit, didn't I sort all that out for you? OK, so give me a couple of days – three tops – and you'll have what you want."

There was silence from the 'phone and then the man said: "Of course, but please be aware that this is your last chance, do you understand?"

"Yes," Marvin said.

The line went dead, leaving Marvin holding the receiver. He slammed it down. They didn't understand, didn't have a fucking clue about his worth to them, about the times he flew to some arse-end of a town to dispose of their latest problem.

He was beyond the seriously pissed off. He ran from the apartment to the big industrial elevator at the end of the corridor and angrily punched the buzzer. He listened as the elevator creaked and groaned slowly up the shaft.

On the street he waved frantically for a cab. Several passed until he managed to attract an empty one. He jumped into the back seat, threw a $20 to the driver and told him to get over to Penn, like now!

Traffic was quickly backing up, a mad disjointed symphony of honking horns, screeching brakes and arm-waving frustration. The cab inched its way through the traffic, the driver hauling at the wheel in search of a side street to speed the journey but running into even more congestion.

Ahead, a large furniture truck was triple-parked for a group of men to manhandle heavy, awkward pieces out of the back, across the pavement, up a flight of steps and into a redstone.

Marvin did not bother checking his watch, he knew he was running out of time.

Rachel had returned to the Amtrak Lounge. The departure of the Lake Shore Limited – stopping at a list of stations she could not keep up with – was announced and she rose to join the line of fellow-passengers making their way to the door.

She saw the time-warp woman join the queue several places ahead as they made their way to the gate.

She showed her ticket and walked along the platform, the train hissing and clanking on her right. She walked past several coaches until she came to the sleeping cars. She showed her ticket to a smiling attendant who pointed further along the train.

She found her coach and walked along the narrow corridor to her sleeper.

The sleeper was small and functional, but an exciting cubicle for Rachel. It had a single chair that folded down into a bunk and to the side of the door she found a narrow cupboard. There was, she discovered, a small table that lifted up from underneath the window and on one wall was a bank of knobs and switches for the video and room temperature.

She worked it out that when the bed was set up there would be a gap of just a couple of inches between it and the curtained, sliding door, it would be quite a feat getting undressed and into bed without sticking her bottom into the corridor. It was, she decided, all very quaint and very exciting.

She took her notebook from the laptop case and lifted it and her case onto a string rack. The corridor was filling with people searching for their sleepers so she let them all get organised and sat on the chair looking out at the platform. When the train moved off she would go exploring.

Marvin tried to work out where he was and how far he was from Penn. The station was a couple of blocks away and there was no chance of his cab finding a clear path to it. He told the driver he'd get out here. He took off along the street, bouncing pedestrians as he went.

The attendant walked along the corridor ensuring that his charges had settled in, pointing out the toilets and showers at the end of the line of sleepers, telling them that tea, coffee and soft drinks would be available at one end of the corridor, that once they got out of Manhattan and along the Hudson the diner would be open for business. The lounge-car would be serving snacks, hot and cold drinks … just ask for anything they might need, his name was Jerome.

Marvin ploughed his way through the crowds in Penn, towards the gates, pushing and shoving anybody that got in his way.

He reached the gate just in time to see the train slowly edge its way out of the station. In frustration he shook the gate and cursed at the alarmed ticket collector safe on the other side.

He turned and stumbled over a suitcase. He lashed out at it and a man jumped from a bench … Marvin's cold glare persuaded him to sit down again.

FIFTEEN

JACKSON Wellman was especially attentive that morning, even to bringing Delta breakfast in bed, with a rose in a thin crystal vase. He discussed with great interest her plans for the next couple of days, suggesting that when he returned from his meeting in Chicago they should take a week off and fly down to their house in Bermuda. They deserved the time off together.

Delta played the game ... what a lovely idea, they hadn't been down to the house for such a long time. She held out her arms and he reached down to embrace her. He would love nothing better than to forget about the damn boring meeting and climb in beside her, so he said. Unfortunately it was a meeting he could not get out of, it might bring a couple more magazines into the Octagon family.

Delta understood, she would love nothing better than for him to climb in beside her, but business was business.

She watched him as he finished combing his hair, moving around the bedroom, adjusting his tie and smoothing down the collar of his elegant English shirt, slipping on the jacket of his immaculate Armani suit. She had to admit he was handsome.

He checked his bag and closed it. He returned to her bed and kissed her, pushing his hand under the covers to stroke her. Damn you, she thought, as she automatically slid her legs apart ... damn you, cheating bastard!

He walked out to the car and headed for the airport where he knew Wendy would already be waiting on the Lear, ever the efficient and well-organised PA, always one step ahead, always loyally looking after her boss.

The 'plane lifted into the clean, cool Denver morning air, banked North through the shimmering heat haze and climbed to its cruising height to leave the Rockies behind and the landscape below to bring its own beauty.

Since it was a short flight, Jackson had given the stewardess the day off. With only the pilot and co-pilot in the flight-deck, he and Wendy were alone.

He walked down the 'plane and held up a square decanter in one hand and a coffee pot in the other. Wendy pointed to the coffee and he poured her a cup, and a Bourbon for himself.

She was wearing a distractingly short skirt that rode up above her knees and a pale blue silk shirt distractingly opened several buttons to reveal the swell of her breasts. He set her coffee on the table in front of her and slipped his hand into the shirt to finger a hardening nipple.

She closed her eyes and moaned softly, then put her hand over his and stopped him, nodding forward to the closed door to the flight-deck.

"Behave yourself," she said, still savouring the tingle he had caused, "We're supposed to be working on important papers, Mr Wellman … what would our gallant crew think?"

Jackson smiled and sat down opposite her: "They'd think I was a lucky son of a bitch to be feeling those magnificent breasts."

She kicked off her shoes, stretched a long leg under the table and rubbed him.

The co-pilot came to tell him they were coming up to Midway Airport and to confirm that a car would be waiting to take them the 25 minutes into the hotel in Chicago.

Jackson thanked him.

Midway, named in honour of the World War Two Battle of Midway, was the Windy City's second airport, serving mostly domestic routes and private flights. Wendy had booked a suite in the Sheraton Hotel and Tower on East North Water Street, overlooking the Chicago River and near the shops, theatres and restaurants of the city centre … not that they planned any theatre trips. Not, indeed, that they planned to be seen much outside the door of their suite.

They travelled light so it took little time to disembark and walk through the airport to the waiting car.

The car dropped them in front of the Sheraton where two porters had a race to grab their luggage and wheel it into the marble and embossed wood lobby. They stopped short of carrying Wendy in after it, but only just.

The suite commanded a magnificent view of the city and Wendy stood at the window, holding aside the curtain to look out over it.

"Are you hungry?" she asked, turning back to Jackson.

"Well not necessarily for food," he said.

"Well, I am. I've had two cups of coffee since I got up this morning. Is there a Room Service menu somewhere?"

He handed her the leather hotel directory standing on the dresser and she flopped down on the bed to leaf through it.

"What a great hotel," she said, holding open the pages of photographs and showing him, "Look, darling, this might be the only chance we get to see them."

"Well, tonight I have lined up at least one special outing, so if you intend to eat something right now make it a sandwich and a cup of tea ... tonight we're taking in a show and a fancy restaurant."

"Now then, Mr Wellman," she said, sliding a hand up her outstretched leg, "You really know how to spoil a lady ... and this lady knows how to spoil you."

Marvin returned, once again, to his apartment, his foul mood made even more so at missing the train. He went to the bathroom and splashed cold water on his face. Still dripping he scrolled through his computer and found a red-eye flight later that evening on a cheap airline to Chicago. He booked a seat ... and this time, you little bitch, the running and chasing ends.

The Lake Shore Limited swayed and hissed its way through Manhattan. Rachel steadied herself along the corridor to where Jerome was lifting soft drinks from a box and putting them into a small freezer. She asked where the lounge-car was and he told her she would find it – couldn't miss it – two coaches straight through.

Passengers had already made their way to the car but she found an empty table and set her notebook and pen on it while she got a beer and a thick, triple-slice ham and cheese sandwich from the little bar at the end of the coach.

She opened the notebook ... and the time-warp woman sat down opposite her, hiding the notebook with an avalanche of carrier bags. When Rachel met Peggy Sue-Moonbeam-Roberta Wazowski who had been to Manhattan to buy her wedding dress.

Jayne gathered her magazines and followed the man from the Acela Lounge across South Street Station forecourt, through the gate to the train. Several other passengers – including four who had come into the Lounge after her – fell in behind to find their coach seats or sleepers.

As she settled into her Roomette, she thought of Brad and of their time together in East Bayport … and she wondered if it had all really happened.

The train jerked into life, creaked forward and built up speed. The Boston-Albany leg of the Limited journey was under way.

Bostonians will naturally give you an argument over which of the two Lake Shore Limited routes to Albany is the more interesting. Their leg, after all, takes in Framingham where the New England Wildflower Association has 400 species of native plants at the Garden in the Woods, and the Springfield home of the famous cowboy rifle, and they'll remind you that it was in Pittsfield where Herman Melville wrote Moby Dick and they haven't even got around to mentioning the Berkshire Mountains.

New Yorkers will indulge all this boasting with a smile. Their leg, they will modestly explain, travels along the wide Hudson River, through beautiful little towns like Yonkers, where Elisha Otis invented the elevator, and Hastings-on-Hudson, where the famous showman Florenz Ziegfeld and his actress wife Billie Burke (the good witch in The Wizard of Oz) lived, and Irvington, named after Washington Irving who created Rip Van Winkle. Then there's always Sing Sing to chill the blood, and across the river West Point to stir the blood and Croton-Harmon, soon-to-be-home of the famous Roberta Wazowski. At which point they'll probably get tired fingering off the winning points and just leave it at that.

Rachel, trapped by her motor-mouth new best friend, began to finger off the towns, longing for Croton-Harmon to embrace Roberta to its warm heart.

She was so trapped that she did not dare make an excuse and flee back to her sleeper lest Roberta follow … she had a terrifying vision of sitting on a San Diego beach with Roberta still chattering about her coming wedding.

If only, Rachel thought, she was one of the Ballymena Wazowski's she might at least get a decent feature out of it. But she fixed a mirthless smile and tried to concentrate on the river scene passing by the windows. The train could still, mercifully, plunge into the water and end the torment.

Jayne paid a brief visit to the lounge-car but only a handful of people were scattered about the tables. She bought a coffee and returned to her sleeper … to think of East Bayport, Charlie's Clam Shack, little wooden toys. And a Boston Legal Eagle.

Marvin caught his bare-essentials flight to O'Hare International with thoughts of bloody revenge in mind. No more chasing, this is where the chase ends.

Cross looked once more at the photograph of Wendy Brewer: good looking dame, nice body, good jugs, the confident gaze of a dame who knew what she wanted and how to get it. But at the end of the day just another job. He put the photograph into his wallet and got ready to drive into Chicago the next morning.

Jackson and Wendy returned to the Sheraton after their evening at the theatre – a touring company indifferently performing How To Succeed In Business – and restaurant.

In their suite Jackson took a long, gift-wrapped box from his case and handed it to her. She tore off the paper to reveal a red leather box. She opened it and lifted out a sparkling diamond pendant on a long gold chain.

"Put it on," Jackson said.

"OK," Wendy said, kissing him, "but let me take a shower first … and then you'll see it."

She stripped and walked to the bathroom. Jackson poured them drinks and relaxed in one of the deep chairs, looking out at the twinkling lights of the city.

Wendy towelled herself and put on her perfume. She lifted the gift and put it around her waist, the diamond falling in an inviting V towards her trimmed curls.

She smiled and walked back to Jackson. She stood in front of him.

"Like it, darling?"

Jackson liked it, very much.

The train from Boston reached Albany-Rensselaer 40 minutes behind schedule, but still ahead of the leg from Penn. Jayne joined the other passengers for a leg-stretch around the station. There was a small, uninteresting gift shop and a coffee corner but she walked outside the station on East Street, actually not in Albany but in Rensselaer, across the Hudson.

Albany was the State Capitol of New York, not, as a lot of people think, New York itself. It was known as the Hidden City, which probably explained a great deal. But then a lot of people think Los Angeles or San Fransisco must be the Capitol of California … nope, it's Sacramento. Nothing in America is ever quite what it seems.

Jayne walked back to the platform and sat on a bench, waiting for Rachel and the Limited from New York. They'd certainly have

139

a lot to chat about.

The train was late but eventually, after another 40 minutes had crept by, it swayed into the station. Jayne got up and looked along the newly-arrived coaches for Rachel.

She spotted her climbing from a coach at the rear of the train and they raced along the platform to embrace like excited schoolgirls, dancing and twirling and laughing.

They babbled excitedly over each other's sentences … what they had been up to since parting at Dublin Airport, who they had met, the sights they had seen.

Jayne flapped her hands to get Rachel to stop talking and walked her back to her friend's Roomette. She sat her down on the bed and held her hands … and she told Rachel all about Brad and East Bayport and Schooner Cove and Barney and Charlie's Clam Shack and Stella and Tony's.

And Rachel listened open-mouthed. And when Jayne had finished her tale Rachel screamed, flung herself across the bed and hugged her friend.

"I can't believe it!"

Then again, neither could Jayne.

SIXTEEN

MARVIN went to the bank of free telephones when he had passed through arrivals and booked a room in a Holiday Inn beside the airport. He would relax – he would, actually, try to calm down, the better to finally finish what was turning into a marathon job – and the following morning he would make his way to Union Station to await Rachel.

And this time he would make no stupid mistakes, his reputation was built on the mistakes he never made ... play it cool, he warned himself, cool and efficient.

Now running from Albany to Chicago as one train, the Limited turned towards the Mid-West.

Rachel and Jayne took themselves to the diner for a meal, all part of the price of their ticket. The train was now running just under one hour behind schedule, but doing its best to make up the time.

The combined train was now clearly full and they were seated with an elderly couple – Marge and Horace, which made Rachel think instantly of Marge and Homer Simpson – going to Toledo to see their new grandson.

The meal finished, they went to the lounge-car for a glass of wine and more excited chatter about Jayne's great romance.

"Oh, by the way," Jayne suddenly remembered, "Amtrak have upgraded us to a Bedroom on the Zephyr, we'll have our own shower all the way to San Fransisco. The people I met in Boston have made all the arrangements."

They watched the countryside roll past as the train hit Syracuse, Rochester and Buffalo, by which time it was dark outside. They retired to grapple with the complexities of getting ready for bed in a three-feet by six-feet box.

Jackson and Wendy awoke at 8.30am, made love again, shared

a scalding shower, made love again and ordered breakfast.

Cross made a call to Denver to let Collins know he was on the move. He shaved, grabbed a quick mug of black coffee and from the cloakroom of his pokey apartment on the far side of O'Hare to downtown Chicago, he removed a shoe-box and took out a gun and a silencer. He tucked the gun into the belt of his jeans and the silencer in a pocket of the black leather jacket he lifted from the back of a chair. He was on the move.

Jackson had a problem. During the night a message had been sent to the hotel … a strike had been called at an Octagon plant outside of Greenwood, Mississippi. He had to get a quick flight out of Chicago to go kick some ass.

He suggested Wendy stay on for a couple of days, do some shopping on State Street, take in the sights.

When he left Wendy decided she would not stay on, it would not be the same without Jackson. She decided to go back to Denver and called reception to ask if they would book her a flight.

Wendy had a problem. The receptionist called back and told her that no seats on any airline would be available until late the following afternoon.

Wendy asked if any seats on anything leaving Chicago were available right now. When reception called back for a second time with possible alternatives Wendy dismissed outright the Greyhound – no way was she going to sit on a bloody bus all the way to Denver – but the overnight run on Amtrak's California Zephyr did not sound too bad. She had not been on a train since she was little girl, it might be fun. OK, she said, book a seat on the train, do whatever was necessary to get her a sleeper as well.

The Limited crawled into Union Station, having pulled back 30 minutes on its overnight trip. For Rachel and Jayne the delay hardly mattered since the Zephyr was not due to depart until around 2pm. They went to the Metropolitan Lounge, sorted out their new sleeping arrangements and found time for a brief exploration around the city, with a quick dash to the top of the Sears Tower for a panoramic view of the city and Lake Michigan.

Cross found traffic surprisingly light as he drove towards the airport, he would make good time into town. But he started to encounter heavy traffic pouring from the airport.

He reached for his cell, better call the Sheraton to confirm the Brewer woman was there. As the hotel was telling him that she had checked out he dropped the cell and bent down to retrieve it.

Marvin got a cab from the Holiday Inn. The traffic was a nightmare, it reminded him of his desperate dash through Manhattan to Penn Station.

"There seems to be an accident ahead," the driver said. They had snarled up in a jam of vehicles just beyond the airport exit. The driver got out and picked his way through the lines of vehicles to the roadside, scanning the road ahead to where he could see a billowing cloud of black smoke.

"Looks bad," he said, getting back into his seat, "But there are plenty of cops up ahead trying to get us moving. Shouldn't take long."

Slowly the vehicles in front began to jerk forward, directed by a policeman in single file past the burning remains of a two cars pileup. Paramedics and ambulances were drawn up around the wreckage, a fire engine pumped foam on the cars and on the road around them.

"Poor bastards," the cab driver said, "Nobody walked away from that."

An hour before the departure of her train Wendy checked in at the Metropolitan Lounge for the Zephyr, showing the confirmation print-out the Sheraton had provided when she left. There was one available Roomette, she was fortunate to get it on what was one of the world's great railway journeys. She felt rather excited about the trip as she settled into a comfortable seat to study the other passengers. Some of them, she discovered, were actually waiting for the Empire Builder to Seattle, away on the Pacific Coast. She had never realised that trains criss-crossed the country to such an extent, with a company Lear to whisk her around she had never been required to.

She would have quite a story to tell Jackson when she met him. Miss Cool Personal Assistant riding the rails, playing hobo.

Marvin walked down the wide stairway from the street, into the cathedral-like general waiting room, with its marble pillars and its polished original wooden benches. The stairs, he remembered, had been used by the director Brian de Palma for the shoot-out scene with the slowly bouncing pram in The Untouchables, the Kevin Costner-Robert De Nero story of local gangster hero Al Capone, his favourite character.

He was careful to select a bench in a far corner of the large waiting area. He knew already that Andrews was travelling on the Zeph-

143

yr and guessed she would be in the Amtrak lounge waiting to board and he did not want the risk of going near it and being seen by her. He would wait where he was and listen for the announcements, then he would board the train himself and wait for the right moment.

Things, he felt, were coming back under his control. He felt better when he was in control.

To his surprise he saw the young reporter coming down the stairs, and she was with another young woman. Keep calm, Marvin told himself, it was probably just somebody she had attached herself to. He watched as they made their way to the lounge.

Jayne found them a seat while Rachel went for a couple of complimentary soft drinks. She waited as a girl in front of her poured a coffee.

When the girl turned she had to do a quick recovery to avoid spilling the coffee over Rachel.

"Oh gee!" she cried, "I'm so damn awkward, are you OK?"

Rachel assured her that no coffee had reached her.

"Are you on the Zephyr?" the girl asked.

"Yes, my friend Jayne and I, that's her over there, are going all the way to California … we're on holiday."

"Gee, I love your accent."

Rachel tried not to cringe, the memory of Roberta Wazowski still fresh in her memory. She smiled and figured she had just better get it over with: she, and Jayne, were from Northern Ireland.

The girl juggled the coffee and held out a hand: "I'm Margaret Carrington– friends call me Mags – I'm only going as far as Denver, that's in Colorado."

"And I'm Rachel Andrews. My friend is Jayne McGregor. If you're on your own why don't you come and join us."

"Thanks, I'd love to," Mags said, executing another death-defying balancing trick with the coffee, "I guess I'd better drink this before somebody gets drowned. I'll get my bag and come over."

She was, she told them when she pulled an empty seat over to join them, going home to visit her family, who lived in Estes Park.

Rachel and Jayne looked baffled and Mags explained: "Oh, Estes Park, well it's a beautiful little town in the Rockies, you'd love it. My mother and two sisters – Amanda is a detective in Estes Park and Beth is a college student in Boulder - have a cabin there, my mother's an artist. I'm a boring accountant in Chicago, so I try to escape back home as often as I can."

Sitting nearby, Wendy caught snatches of the conversation and smiled to herself. She too loved Estes Park but because Jackson and Delta had a house – The Hall, no less -there she seldom got to visit the town. Perhaps one day she too would live there.

Marvin listened to the announcements and joined the end of the queue of passengers moving to the gate. Now, he noted, there were bloody three of them, what was it with Andrews?

The sleeper passengers trooped along the platform and he pulled himself up and into the nearest coach, walking through it and the next one until he found his seat. He sat down ... now all he had to do was watch and wait and, somewhere down the line, move.

Mags had a sleeper two coaches along from Rachel and Jayne so they arranged to meet in the lounge car after the girls had explored their Bedroom. It was much the same as their single cabins – measuring six by seven it was not much larger - but it had a toilet and shower and a chair that didn't need wrestling into a bunk. They tossed for the top bunk – Jayne won – stowed their luggage and just as the train rattled into its long journey across the West they bounced excitedly along the corridor to meet up with Mags.

Wendy found her Roomette quaint, the bunk adequate, her fellow-travellers the usual odd-ball mix, the experience full of possibilities. It wasn't the Octagon Lear but for a quick overnighter it looked like a lot of fun.

In his coach seat Marvin tried to get comfortable, surrounded by complaining children and nerve-shredded adults. He poured over a timetable, trying to work out where might be the best place for his move. If the train kept to its schedule he figured somewhere between Omaha and Hastings. The timetable gave 1.57am as the arrival time for Hastings, allow for a more than probably delay and he might be able to get Andrews off the train and away.

OK, so there have been better prepared plans but he was running out of more plausible options. Anyway, he determined to make it work.

In Denver, Collins called Delta to keep her up to date: Cross had called him earlier and was on his way.

Rachel and Jayne were given a horoscope-free, crystal-free and amusing commentary by Mags as the train went through Naperville and Princeton and Galesburg until they decided it was time for dinner.

Wendy had taken a constitutional pre-dinner walk from one end of the train to the other, amazed at the confusion and noise in the seating-only coaches that were already littered with discarded newspapers, magazines and coffee containers, the aisles turned into race tracks by excited children, the seats filled with sprawling, chattering passengers, some trying to doze, others playing cards.

She joined the line waiting outside the restaurant car to be seated, following the attendant past the girls she had seen in the station to a table already occupied by a silent woman and a young couple. Thankfully, aside from the initial smiles and nods of the heads, she was not required to play the game that people who will never see one another ever again seem compelled to play when thrown together on a long journey: no life stories necessary.

The attendant moved along the car and handed her a slip of paper and a stubby pensil and she wrote down the meal she would like: soup, Basil and Thyme Cod, creamed potatoes, a bottle of white wine, a slice of cheesecake and a coffee. Maybe it was because she was just hungry, but she rather enjoyed it.

She lingered over the meal until the train pulled out of Osceola and went back to her sleeper.

Marvin debated going for a coffee but wasn't sure if it would be a wise move. Stuck with the rabble in coach hell he did not want to risk running into Rachel. He figured by now she'd have gathered around her a small platoon of females. On the other hand, he thought, she wouldn't recognise him, had she ever seen him before in her life?

He excused himself and squeezed past the man sitting beside him. He picked his way across the forest of legs stretched into the aisle and walked to the lounge. Thankfully it was almost empty. He bought a coffee and a thick ham and cheese sandwich and made his way back to his seat.

As darkness fell and the coach settled into a collective restless slumber, the main lights of the coach having been dimmed leaving only spotlights of overhead seat beams, the train, 30 minutes late, stopped at Omaha, Nebraska.

He took a quick look at the crumpled piece of paper he had brought from New York then carefully negotiated his way past his snoring companion and walked to the end of the carriage, where the attendant was closing the door. He waited until the attendant had gone and continued towards the sleeper coaches.

Several of the newly-boarded passengers were sorting themselves out at their various little boxes as he eased past. Nobody took any interest in him.

Three coaches along he found the one he was looking for. The corridor was empty, but just as he was about to walk along it a door opened. He slid quickly out of sight as a woman went to the far end and returned to her sleeper holding a bottle of spring water. He listened as she slid the door closed and clicked the lock.

He checked off the numbers of the Bedrooms and came to the one he wanted. He scanned the corridor one more time and tapped gently on the door.

As soon as he heard the lock being lifted, Marvin slipped his hand around the door and slid it open. He stepped into the Bedroom and slapped the occupant across the face. She fell back across the bunk, her head striking the metal surrounding the window with a crunch. He pulled the door closed behind him and grabbed her by the throat. She looked at him, tears and terror in her glazed eyes.

"Shit!" Marvin said.

He pulled her from the bed and felt the blood seeping from the sticky gash on the back of her head. He grabbed her hair, put his arm around her neck and jerked her head. He heard the crack.

He pulled back the bedclothes and laid her out, pulling them up to her chin. He wiped the door where he had pushed it open, checked the corridor – it was still silent and empty – and closed the door.

At the end of the corridor he stumbled into the washroom and splashed cold water on his face, palming water into his dry mouth. He gazed at his reflection in the mirror and thumped the wall.

"Shit! Shit!"

He slipped off the train at Hastings.

Rachel and Jayne slept soundly but they simply could not contain their excitement, so they lay at either end of the bottom bunk with the blind up looking out at the Colorado scenery.

The train was crawling slowly through an endless cattle yard filled with endless rows of cattle pens towards Denver. Off to their right they could see the blue-gray outline of the Rockies drifting in a cloak of morning mist. It was exactly what they had imagined it to be: mountains and cows.

Rachel pulled herself reluctantly from the scenery and took a shower. Jayne smiled and remembered the alternate showers another world away. Without realising it, she was clutched a pillow.

She was curious about the line of police cars that began to appear alongside the track, their blue, red and white lights twinking on and off.

She called to Rachel: "They must have warned Denver you were passing through, seems the police have turned up to keep the citizens safe."

"What?"

"Come and take a look, there are police cars everywhere."

Rachel wrapped a towel around her and, drying her hair, joined Jayne at the window. The train was still swaying towards the station and outside she could see the cars.

"It's more likely you they're here for," she said, poking Jayne, "Ready to keep you away from handsome Denver lawyers. I wonder what it's all about, though."

"Looks quite serious," Jayne said, "Anyway, my turn for the shower … and then a hearty breakfast. Train travel does wonders for my appetite."

Rachel dressed in a New York Mets sweat she had treated herself to and a pair of jeans and watched the activity outside until the train arrived at Denver station.

They answered the knock on their Roomette door and opened it to see their attendant standing in the corridor with a policeman.

"What's happened?" Jayne asked.

"There was an accident back along the line, miss," the policeman said, "We need to talk to the passengers. You're going through to San Fransisco, I believe, so we'll try not to delay you too much, but we do need to talk to everybody, especially the sleeper car passengers."

The attendant gave them a reassuring smile: "Your things will be safe, I'll look after them, but if you get ready the officer will escort you to the station. There's nothing to worry about."

They followed the policeman out of the coach and joined the other passengers milling about on the platform.

"What happened, does anybody know?" Rachel asked a group of passengers.

"Not sure," one of them offered, "but I overheard our attendant talking to one of the cops, seems a woman was found dead in one of the sleepers."

"Dead!" Rachel said.

"Yep, dead as in murdered," another of the group said.

The police were full of apologies as they formed the passengers into two lines stretching back from the station terminal.

Rachel and Jayne looked along both lines.

"I don't see Mags, wasn't she in one of the sleepers?" Jayne asked.

"Yes, she was in a single Bedroom a couple of coaches up from us. I can't see her either," Rachel said, stepping out from the line to look for Mags, "It's chaos ... they're still trying to get the queues in order."

Inside the big, square Union Station, with its rows of long bench-seats, pairs of policemen were questioning passengers.

When it was their turn, a plainclothes detective escorted them to one of the benches where a uniformed policewoman sat writing in a notebook. She smiled and asked them to take a seat.

She explained what, as far as knew, had happened: the attendant in one of the sleeper cars had gone to waken a Denver-bound passenger with an early morning coffee and newspaper and had found her in her bunk, blood had seeped and congealed around her head and it looked like somebody had broken her neck. The Zephyr crew had called ahead ... which was why Denver Station was crawling with police.

"Do you have a name?" Rachel asked.

"A name?"

Rachel explained that they had met and befriended a girl in Chicago who was travelling to Denver, her name was Margaret Carrington. They hadn't seen her standing outside.

The policewoman flicked back through her notebook: "They haven't given us the name of the victim yet, we're pretty far down the food chain. So no news is good news."

They told the policewoman their names, filled in what they were doing in the USA, what they had been doing, especially since leaving Chicago. It seemed to satisfy their questioner.

"If you don't mind, please don't leave the station until we give the all clear," she told them, "If I were you I'd grab a coffee and go sit outside on the platform. When we find your friend I'll tell her where you are, OK?"

They thanked her and did what they were told. Jayne took a coffee back to the grateful policewoman.

They walked along the platform to the front of the train and found a quiet spot to sit down.

Other bemused passengers, freed from their own interrogations,

149

found their way along the platform, clutching hot and cold drinks to cluster around them and talk about what had happened.

One woman seemed to have more information than the others: "I was getting off here, I live in Denver. My husband is outside waiting to collect me.

"It's just awful what's happened. I know the dead woman ... well, I don't know her personally but I know of her. She works – worked – for a big company in Denver, she was the private secretary, something like that, of the man who owns it.

"I've seen her picture in the local 'papers a couple of times. She was very glamorous."

The group wondered why anybody would want to murder her? Even more chilling, they wondered who had murdered her and if they were even now walking around the platform? They glanced suspiciously at one another.

A tinny station announcement asked the passengers to assemble inside and when they had settled themselves around the benches and along the walls a voice echoed from the speakers.

"My name is John Brand and I'm a Captain with the Denver Police Department. I'd like to thank you all for your co-operation, I hope you understand we have to obtain as much information as we can.

"Anyway, we will now have to remove the coach where the body was found from the train. It's now a crime scene ...," he tried a lame joke, " ... all you fans of CSI can explain what I mean to the others.

"The train conductor and crew will take all of you who were in Coach E back to collect your things ... and please don't get in the way of our people you'll see there. Amtrak will do their best to accommodate you in any other available sleepers," he appeared to be interrupted briefly and then he came back on, "OK, I've just been told they will have a new coach to replace the one we're removing up the line at Glenwood Springs or at Salt Lake City.

"We'll have you sorted out as soon as we can ..." again he was interrupted, "OK, even better. The crew will be giving out complimentary snacks shortly. Guess if all else fails I can always get a job on the railway."

The passengers filed out to the platform again and as they walked back to their spot Rachel and Jayne heard Mags call their name. They turned and waited as she raced towards them and hugged them.

"We were looking for you," Rachel said.

"And I was looking for you," Mags said, sitting down, "A policewoman told me where you were, just before the announcement. What a terrible thing to have happened. I've actually heard of Wendy Brewer, she's from here."

She got up: "Don't go away, would you believe it: I was in the coach they'll be taking away. I have to go get my bag. My sister Amanda is probably stuck out on Wynkoop Street, that's where this station is, waiting for me."

They shared another group hug and Mags raced off.

"It's all happening," Rachel said as they sat down.

"I'm glad Amtrak up-graded us to a Roomette, all we have to do is wait here until they give the train the all clear," Jayne said.

"I forgot about that," Rachel said ... then she frowned, "What coach did they say they were keeping?"

Jayne thought for a moment: "E I think it was. Yes it was E. Why?"

Rachel shuddered: "We were supposed to be in Coach E, don't you remember? Then they gave us the Roomette."

Jayne tried to recall what coach it had been but couldn't.

"I even remember the Bedroom number I got," Rachel said.

She got up suddenly: "Keep our place, Jayne, I have to talk to that policewoman. I won't be long."

Inside the station, now with only the last remnants of the passengers being questioned, she searched for the policewoman and eventually saw her comparing notes with four other officers. She caught her attention and the policewoman excused herself from the group and came over.

"Sorry for bothering you," Rachel said, "but could you tell me the number of the Bedroom they found the woman in?"

"I'm sorry but I'm not allowed to give out information. Is there any particular reason why you want to know?"

"OK, I understand," Rachel said, "Well then, can I give you a number and if it's the same one ...?

"I don't understand."

"Was it 11, Bedroom 11, Coach E?"

The policewoman looked at her and then opened her notebook. She looked again at Rachel, this time with interest.

"Would you mind coming with me, Miss Andrews?" she said.

Concerned, Rachel fell in beside the policewoman and was led through the curious, glaring remaining passengers to a room at the front of the station and asked to wait inside.

Rachel sat at a square pine table stained with rings from hot mugs and cigarette burns and nervously examined the fading notices on the dirty cream walls warning her of the rules and regulations regarding working for the National Railroad Passenger Corporation. There was a torn poster of a snow-capped peak welcoming her to scenic Colorado … yeah, thanks a lot! And they say Americans don't do irony.

Outside on the platform a disturbing rumour began to spread that the police had arrested a passenger and were now probably getting to the truth with the aid of night-sticks.

Jayne and Mags, now sitting with her legs over her retrieved bag, exchanged glances.

The policewoman returned to the depressing room with a colleague. They sat across the table from Rachel and the man introduced himself as Captain John Brand. Rachel decided not to comment that she wished he had gone to work for Amtrak.

"The officer tells me you should have been in 11/E," he said, "Can you tell us why you weren't, miss?"

Rachel explained about her friend Jayne being given the upgrade by Amtrak.

"And why would they do that?" the policewoman asked.

"I don't really know," Rachel said, "Perhaps Jayne, she's the girl you interviewed with me, she's out on the platform, could tell you."

The policewoman looked at the Captain who nodded. She left the room to bring back Jayne.

"Did you know Miss Brewer?" the Captain wondered.

"No, not at all," Rachel said.

Outside on the platform the policewoman found Jayne and asked if she would come with her.

"Why?" Jayne asked.

"Just some routine questions. You have no objection?" the policewoman said, narrowing her eyes to show that the question might be construed as such.

Jayne got up and, with Mags tagging along, the trio returned down the platform through more curious and glaring passengers.

Rachel looked relieved when her friends were shown into the room, now at least she did not feel quite so alone.

"Your friend here says it was you who changed your sleeping arrangements, could you explain?" the Captain said.

"Well, it wasn't me as such," Jayne began, "it was Amtrak. I'm researching a possible series of radio programmes on Amtrak for the BBC back home and I had a meeting with some of their people in Boston. Rachel and I had booked the two singles before we left home but Amtrak thought we would like to be together in a Roomette … it has a shower."

"I see," the Captain, "and I'm sure Amtrak will confirm all this?"

Jayne shrugged, she assumed they would be able to.

He turned his attention back to Rachel: "Who else knew about this?"

"Excuse me?"

"Who else knew you had been up-graded? Anybody, for instance, in New York?"

Rachel thought: "I don't know: Amtrak knew, of course, and Jayne. Actually, I didn't know until Jayne told me when we met at Albany."

"Albany?" the policewoman asked.

She obviously wasn't aware of the two-leg Lake Shore Limited, probably wasn't even aware there was such an animal as a Lake Shore Limited, which did sound rather like a small, endangered furry creature. They explained and the policewoman wrote it all down as though she felt she had cracked the case.

"Did you know the murdered woman?" she asked Jayne.

"No."

The policewoman snorted a hmmph!

"And you, miss …" the Captain looked at Mags.

"We just met while waiting for the train in Chicago. I'm here to sort of lend moral support."

"Did you know …"

"Well, my family live in Estes Park so I guess I've heard of Wendy Brewer. Hasn't everybody?"

The Captain threw another glance at his officer. Then they rose from the table.

"If you don't mind waiting," he said.

When they were left alone Jayne asked what had happened.

"When you remembered we were originally supposed to be in Coach E I remembered I was originally in Bedroom 11, that's where the dead woman was found," Rachel said.

"My God!" Mags said, "What does that mean?"

They pondered the question.

"It just means what it seems," Jayne said, "I wouldn't read too much into it."

Jayne and Mags decided to lift the gloom.

"Except," Mags suggested, "you'll have to get used to an orange boiler-suit ..."

"Smashing big rocks on a dusty road ..."

"Fending off the advances of a large, butch woman with a moustache ..."

"You two aren't funny," Rachel said, "This is serious. They think I had something to do with all this."

"We'll bring you a file in a fruit-cake," Mags said, patting Rachel's hand.

"There are enough fruit-cakes here already, so enough of the jokes. What's going to happen now?"

Before they could decide what might happen the Captain returned and sat down.

"I'm afraid I'm going to have to ask you to stay in Denver until we look into the matter. I know all this must be upsetting for you and I assure you we'll try and get you on your way as quickly as we can, but we do need to keep you here."

He got up: "Now, if you don't mind going with my officer, she's waiting for you outside, and getting your stuff from the train."

Rachel and Jayne walked silently with the policewoman to their Roomette and packed their cases. They carried them back to the station, the passengers parting to let them through.

"God," Rachel whispered to Jayne, "They all think I'm Lizzie Borden. I've never been so embarrassed in my life."

Jayne put an arm around her friend's shoulder and hugged her.

"No they don't, they're just confused and frustrated. Anyway, they probably never heard of Lizzie Borden."

They were left alone with Mags in the room.

"Where are we going to stay in Denver? We don't know anybody here," Rachel said.

"Well, I don't live in Denver," Mags said, "but you know me. Just wait here, I think I have the answer."

She left the room and outside she looked for Captain Brand.

"Can I have a word, Captain," she said, taking him aside from some policemen he was chatting to.

"Look," she explained, "The girls had nothing to do with what happened, you must realise that. They have never been in Denver in their lives and don't know anybody here.

"But my family live in Estes Park. I know it's a fair way away but I could take them there. At least that way they won't be on their own."

He considered this for some minutes and then Mags remembered her sister.

"Oh, my sister, she's probably still waiting for me outside, she's with the Estes Park police. If you speak to her she will vouch for Rachel and Jayne. I can bring them back here whenever you need to talk to them. You can't just leave them stranded in Denver not knowing anybody."

"OK," he said, "Go with the officer and find your sister. Bring her back here and I'll talk to her."

Mags and the policewoman walked out to Wynkoop Street. The street was full of TV vans and reporters lined up in front of Union Station babbling their reports. A crowd had been herded behind police tape.

"Can you see her?" the policewoman asked, scanning the throng.

Mags looked around the crowd and saw Amanda waving to her.

"There she is, over on the left," Mags waved back and Amanda pushed towards her.

"Amanda's your sister?" the officer said, "I know her, we were at the Academy together."

When Amanda got to them she smiled and hugged the officer and Mags, who explained what had happened and about Rachel and Jayne as they returned to the station.

Amanda and the Captain stood together and she nodded throughout the conversation.

The Captain walked over to Mags: "It's all arranged. I'll probably get chewed out for it, but your friends can go to Estes Park, just as long as they check in daily with the local police."

Amanda returned to explain to Rachel and Jayne what she had arranged. While they were waiting, Mags had called her mother in Estes Park to tell her about the two guests.

Amanda led them to her pick-up – one of the models with a

155

four-seat cabin. They humped the cases into the back and headed for the Rockies.

SEVENTEEN

DELTA sat on the lawn that rolled down from the Estes Park house to a narrow, gurgling river – more of a stream with ambitions – and sipped a cold orange juice. The morning held the promise of another late June-early July Rockies summer with its soothing breeze from the surrounding mountains rustling a sweet symphony through the trees.

She loved this time of the year. Hay, she loved any time of the year in Estes Park, at the house, pottering along the main street with its boutiques and art galleries and book shops and cafes. The streets were always full of wide-eyed visitors enjoying the delights of the beautiful little town tucked into the valley. Who would not love Estes Park?

This morning Delta felt particularly happy. Jackson had been especially loving when he had called the night before. He was, apparently, missing her, was still talking about that trip to the Bermuda house.

He was still down in Greenwood, still wrestling with the strike at the Mississippi plant. He was in fractious negotiations with Union representatives but, not to worry, darling, he was making progress. He figured the little local difficulty would be resolved in a couple of days and he'd fly back to her loving arms.

But that was not what was making Delta happy. What she was listening to on KCFR AM was the reason for her contentment.

An excited, breathless reporter was standing outside Union Station in downtown Denver with another news up-date on the tragic events that had overtaken the California Zephyr.

A police spokesman – the reporter introduced him as Captain John Brand from the DPD, who was in charge of the investigation – had told her, EXCLUSIVELY, that the woman found dead in one of the sleepers had been identified as Wendy Brewer, who worked for Octagon Enterprises in Denver.

Police, naturally, were following up several strong leads and were preparing to make an arrest very soon.

Like hell, they are, Delta thought. Strong leads being followed up and arrests about to be made meant they had diddly-squat.

The reporter threw in some background on the tragic victim: well liked Personal Assistant to the head of Octagon Enterprises, Jackson Wellman, the scion of Colorado society with his beautiful wife Delta Dubette-Wellman.

She walked back into the house and switched on the television to KCNC4. Another blonde, toothy and smiling reporter– come on you stupid dame, it's a murder you're covering not a society wedding, what's with the vapid smile – was standing with Union Station and a crowd of ghouls as a suitable background.

Much the same guff as her radio colleague had been giving out, and again with the EXCLUSIVE runner scrolling across the bottom of the screen: tragic event, glamorous victim, well known, police ready to swoop.

Delta wondered if the tragic news had filtered through to Jackson down in Greenwood. She wondered if she should call him herself. She decided not to, not just yet. She wanted to savour the moment.

The thing that surprised her was that Wendy had been on the train. Why was she on the train? Delta knew, from Jackson, that Wendy had to stay behind in Chicago when he was called urgently to Greenwood, to, so he said, wrap up the paperwork on the takeover bid. He had grabbed a flight to Mississippi. Why was Wendy using the train?

Collins had called to say Cross was heading into Chicago, so he must have found out Wendy had caught the Zephyr.

Minor points, anyway, Delta told herself. Cross had earned his fee. It would soon be Jackson's turn. Delta took a pile of magazines into the garden, she was feeling good.

As she settled into her favourite wicker chair, the sun beaming down on her, her cell trilled. She picked it and flicked it open.

"It's Collins …"

Delta interrupted him: "Your man did a good job, I've been listening to the news …"

"Well," Collins cleared his throat before continuing, "that's the thing. My man didn't make it; he didn't, er, do the job."

Delta sat up: "What do you mean, it's all over the news?"

"I know it is, I know your problem has been taken care of … but not by Cross."

"How do you know that?"

"Because I just got a call from Chicago," Collins said, "Cross was on his way into town to meet with your, er, problem … but he had an accident …"

"An accident?"

"Yes, he was in a smash-up near the airport," Collins said, "Cross was killed … actually he was fried to a crisp when his gas tank blew. I don't know who took care of your problem, but it wasn't Cross."

Curious, Delta thought.

Four other passengers had got out at Hastings. Marvin followed them out onto West First Street where they got into a beat-up Olds and chugged off in a cloud of black smoke.

He walked around the side of the station and found a solitary Veterans cab. The driver was asleep at the wheel, his head thrown uncomfortably back against the head-rest, his mouth gaping open. He wrapped on the window and the driver jerked awake, amazed that anybody would actually require his services, and glared out at him. He rolled down the window and eyed Marvin with a suspicious squint.

"Any decent hotels, motels in this place?" Marvin asked.

"Sure, we got plenty," the driver said with the air of a native anxious to defend his home town, "You just off the train?"

Marvin climbed in the back. It was the middle of the fucking night, the train had just arrived and was taking off again: where else would he have come from?

"Yeah," he said, "Just get me to a decent hotel, OK?"

The driver shrugged: "Best Western up left on West 33rd is OK."

He watched Marvin in his mirror as he steered through the deserted streets.

"You didn't have any luggage," he said as casually as he could.

"I travel light."

The driver shrugged again: takes all sorts.

Marvin paid him and walked into the motel, explaining to the barely-interested receptionist why he had no luggage: car packed in outside town.

He took the key and went to his room.

He lay on the bed and went over the events of the evening. It wasn't Andrews he had found in the sleeper, but some sexy looking dame. He might have thought up some lame excuse about mistaking her Bedroom for his own and beat a hasty retreat but after he had slapped her and she had fallen against the window she had looked at him. He couldn't risk her remembering him when the attendant and the cops arrived on the scene.

He heaved a self-pitying sigh: a fucking cock-up, ANOTHER fucking cock-up. The Andrews bitch was proving to be his jinx, every time he tried to get near her it turned to shit. And now he'd lost her completely, she was somewhere between here and San Fransisco … the hell he was going all the way to San Fransisco. Maybe the associates were right, maybe he'd be better off agreeing that she didn't know anything about the money.

Maybe he'd just find the nearest airport and go home to New York.

He fell asleep on top of the bed and didn't waken until 9.15am. He felt like death warmed up, his clothes sticky with sweat. He stripped and took a cold shower, he fingered the stubble on his chin and desperately longed for a shave.

Even more desperate was his desire to get the hell out of Hastings, Neb-fucking-raska. He threw his underwear and socks into the white plastic bin liner in the bathroom and slipped on his shirt, trousers and shoes. In the motel lobby he picked up a copy of the Hastings Tribune and flicked through it searching for a clothes shop.

The town was, he discovered, in the heartland of the rich agricultural Nebraska hinterland. Like he gave a fuck. It was also the proud site of the Softball Hall of Fame. Like he gave a ditto!

He walked into the shopping area and found a store selling sturdy agricultural work clothes. He bought and changed into a pair of jeans, a checked shirt and a pair of thick woollen socks. He hit the street looking like a horny-handed yokel.

He found a fast-food outlet – Big Al's All-Nite Diner – sat at a formica table and got a coffee and doughnut from the fortysomething bleached blonde waitress with Joleen taped across her not-for-real-surely knockers. She made with the hi-tall-stranger-in-town smile, he made with the get-lost-bitch scowl and she stomped off.

He laid the Tribune across the table but found nothing of interest in it, nothing to get the juices of a New Yorker flowing.

With nothing better to do, he gave Hastings a chance to endear itself to him. It made such a good effort that, to his amazement, he decided to stay for one more night ... hay, what had he to go back to: more grief from the associates? That he did not need.

He tried not to look like a schmuck as he hit the Places of Interest he found listed in a tourist brochure he picked up at the library.

He bought some additional, more stylish, clothes, a packet of razors, a can of foam and an overnight bag and took them back to the Best Western. He took a hot shower and shave and fell asleep on the bed.

The Tribune he picked up the following morning had the full story, and it decided his next move.

Since Octagon Enterprises had a fertiliser plant on the outskirts of Hastings and since the town was one of the Amtrak stops before Denver, the newspaper had a local interest to go big with. Not only was there a photograph of Wendy Brewer – she was a sexy dame, Marvin thought without pity – there was one of the plant with an inset of some dude captioned Jackson Wellman.

But what caught Marvin's attention was a photograph of Andrews and the two broads he'd seen her with in Chicago taken outside Denver Union ... flanked by a female cop and another broad. A sidebar said that two British citizens had been taken from the train and were helping police with their investigation.

He sat back: so Andrews wasn't on her happy way to California, she was in Denver. Marvin allowed himself a smile.

He walked outside and put his network to use. He called a friend in Denver – in the same line of business as himself – and asked him to find out where the local cops were holding Andrews.

He looked for a rental depot and hired a car. He found a map of Nebraska-Colorado in the side pocket and studied it. He realised he might as well be looking at a map of Mars, he had not a single clue how to get from Hastings to Denver.

Carefully he traced a route – OK, so there might have been a faster way to get to the Mile High City but he figured if he kept to the Amtrak towns along the way he would eventually get there.

Also he wanted to give his contact time to track down Andrews, to find out why she and her two companions had been taken into custody. A not-too-frantic trip would do just fine.

Ever onward, he told himself, go West young man: to McCook, Stratton, over the Stateline to Wray, Fort Morgan and Denver ... go and put an end to his jinx.

It was shortly after he had passed Stratton that his cell tinkled. He pulled off the road to take the call. It was from his contact in Denver. He scribbled the information on the back of a slip of paper he found in the glove compartment.

By now Marvin knew some of what he was being told. The Andrews broad, his contact explained, was originally ticketed to the single Bedroom 11/Coach E but she and her companion had been, for some reason, upgraded and the vacant sleeper sold to a Wendy Brewer, who had been found murdered.

"Anything to do with you?" the contact wanted to know.

"Just get on with it," Marvin snapped.

"OK," the contact continued, "The cops in Denver haven't arrested Andrews as such but they figure she might be indirectly involved in the killing, maybe even the intended target.

"Anyway, until they sort it all out – I'm told they don't reckon on more than three or four days, five tops – they've told Andrews and her friend to stick around."

"And they're still in Denver?" Marvin asked.

"No."

"What the fuck you mean no ... so where are they?"

"That photo you saw in the newspaper: one of the dames with Andrews and her friend is a cop – she was meeting her sister off the train, the other dame – and she's apparently vouched for them and been allowed to take them to Estes Park ..."

Marvin felt the onset of a headache as he tried to keep up with the story.

"Estes Park? Where the fuck is Estes Park?"

"Up in the Rockies, about an hour from here."

"Great, just great. And you're absolutely certain they're in this Estes Park? I need to know. I don't intend to waste time fucking around the foothills."

"Yes, they're in Estes Park. Hold on ..." the contact disappeared briefly and then came back on, "the cop is an Amanda Carrington, she lives in Estes."

Marvin muttered a thanks and before pulling back onto the road took a look at his map. He had difficulty locating Estes Park but eventually found it, stuck in the middle of nowhere surrounded by mountains.

The Octagon Lear flew to Greenwood and delivered Jackson back to Denver late on the evening of the discovery of Wendy's body. When he was given the news he used it to his advantage in the dispute at the Greenwood plant: he was going home, get back to work or he'd shut the plant and move it to India or China.

He met with senior company officials in Denver, talked on the telephone to his good friend the Police Chief and was given an update. He called Delta at Estes Park and she made all the right noises – she was distraught, such a lovely young woman, such a great asset to Jackson – and asked when he was coming home. He decided it would be the right thing to do it right now. He threw in a kiss and a love-you.

Delta was not, particularly, distraught. The only thing that caused her a small distress was that the man her man Collins had contracted to see off Brewer hadn't done it. He had, instead, managed to get himself killed. She couldn't figure it out, though she did concede that the deed done by any other means was still the deed done.

She called Collins to see if he had discovered anything more. He hadn't. She advised him to take off somewhere for a couple of weeks – Florida, New York, California, Anywhere – and, above all, to keep her out of it.

She acted the role of the consoling wife when an ashen and fatigued Jackson arrived. She hugged him and once again ran through the litany of poor Wendy's passing. She poured him a drink and took his hand to lead him out to the darkening lawn.

The best time, she decided, to hit a man was when he was down.

"What was Wendy doing on that train?" she began.

"What?"

"The train ... why was she on the train?"

Jackson shrugged.

"She travelled all over with you, didn't she? She was in Chicago with you, so why didn't she go to Greenwood with you? Such a valuable and loyal employee ..."

Again Jackson shrugged.

"I had to rush away, there was a strike ..."

"But," she persisted, warming up, "you never seemed to be far from her, you couldn't make a decision without her, you ..."

163

"For Christ sake, Delta. I don't know why she was on the train. I left her in Chicago, just that …"

"Left her in your bed."

He jerked his head towards Delta, silently forming words he could not speak.

"I'm not quite the fool you take me for," she said calmly, "so please don't insult me. I've known for some time that you and the wonderful, loyal, hard working Wendy Brewer have been screwing. How long did you imagine you could keep it from me?"

He struggled to concoct a defence, to tell her she was being hysterical, that there was no truth to her allegations … but he couldn't.

"I want you out of the house, tonight," Delta said, "I don't give a damn where you go, just go! And I want you out of the company … I'll be calling a Board meeting in a couple of days and I want your letter of resignation on the table …"

"My God, Delta," Jackson moved towards her but stopped when he saw her face, "This isn't the right time … Wendy has been murdered. And the company …"

"Will go on without you. Don't forget I own the majority stock and the others will do whatever I ask, they wouldn't dare do otherwise, risk losing the fat dividends, the perks they don't have to work for. All they'll need reminding of is what would happen to their lives if I took your sordid little gropings to the press. One hint of that and they'll fall over themselves to collect for your going-away watch. Sorry to see you go, here's your hat and there's the door.

"And where do you think you'd be if I tell the press? Running another corporation, screwing another little whore? Flipping burgers in a cheap all-niter, that's where. The good times just ended tonight.

"And don't forget I am the daughter of 'Bull' Dubette … and I intend to run the company, end of the argument.

"I will keep this house, the New York apartment and the Bermuda house. You can take one of the cars and … no, I guess that's it."

He tried again: "But you nee …"

She held up a dismissive hand: "What? I need you, is that what you were going to say?"

He stared silently at her.

"You need me, but don't for a single second think I need you," she continued, "The first event I go to, without you, there'll be a dozen Jackson Wellmans hanging on my every word. And, believe me, I'll need them even less than I need you. That's the really tragic part of it all, you really do think that I need you."

Delta got up slowly and slapped him hard across his face: "You threw it all away, you bastard!"

She walked back into the house and closed and locked the door.

She watched him from the bedroom window, still slumped on the chair. She gathered all his clothes, all the Armani suits, the London shirts, the silk ties, the Italian shoes, the specially ordered, handmade boxers, the Scottish-knit socks, the gold and silver cuff-links, everything she could find and took them to window. She threw them out, watching as they twisted and fluttered around him, danced across the lawn like ghosts.

In the morning he had gone, along with all the thrown clothes.

EIGHTEEN

THERE are no scenic routes in Colorado. Rather there are no routes in Colorado more scenic than any other, thus every route you take in Colorado is a scenic route, offering another canyon around the next bend, a mountain dressed in pine and aspen, lapped by a river, bordering a lake, watched over by swooping falcons.

Amanda, at the wheel, and Mags beside her in the front of the pick-up, guided the still somewhat bemused Rachel and Jayne around downtown Denver and West towards Boulder, heading towards the rapidly approaching Rockies and Estes Park, their new home for how long they did not know.

Colorado Highway Seven became Arapahoe Road when they reached Boulder and turned North on 15th Street to Canyon Boulevard, State Highway 119 and travelled into Boulder Canyon.

It was magnificent – as were the small canyons and valleys that followed – but it was merely a tantalising trailer for what was to come. Marvin was sort-of right about Estes Park being in the middle of nowhere but utterly wrong in thinking that nowhere was where you would not want to be.

As they climbed up a steep road to crest the hill the town spread out below them, stretching along the Big Thompson River on the front range of the Rocky Mountains. It was the gem of the Rockies, the gateway to the Eastern Rocky Mountain National Park with its North, South and East bordering the Roosevelt National Forest.

Amanda stopped the truck and they got out to look down into the valley, glancing from the lake along the river and the streets.

The town had, Mags explained, been founded in 1859 by Joel Estes and it had grown over the years to become one of the State's, the country's, most popular Summer and Winter resorts, famous for its outdoor pursuits.

But, of course, Joel Estes hadn't been the first human to appreciate the area, for thousands of years the Ute and Arapahoe had treated it as the perfect place for that well-earned vacation break.

"It's my favourite place on Earth," Amanda said, "I've had opportunities to join the Denver Police Department, offered many times, and even to go North to Chicago and New York, but I only have to walk through it, talk to the people, look at the mountains around it, and know I could never leave Estes Park," she laughed, "My God, how soppy that sounds, but damn it I mean it!"

And they could see why, and see why Mags always thought of it rather than Chicago as home.

"OK, hop in and we'll take you to the old homestead," Amanda said and they piled back into the pick-up and took off down towards the town.

Half-way down they swerved left onto a dirt-track road that cut through an avenue of tall trees, bouncing happily alongside a narrow stream.

Suddenly Mags shouted with excitement: "Oh boy, look at this!"

Amanda stopped and they rolled down the windows and leaned out. Coming towards them on the far side of the track in single file were three coyotes. The first two paid no attention to the human intruders but as the third came alongside he stopped and eyed them suspiciously. He had the look of having spent a fruitful morning up to no good ... he twisted his head to one side to indicate that they would hardly credit the places he'd been and the things he'd seen. So, it's what coyotes do. He rolled a pink tongue around his snout, snorted a curt dismissal and loped off to rejoin his fellow travellers.

"Oh, how absolutely brilliant!" Rachel said.

"They're all around the mountains. Don't they look positively naughty?" Mags said.

"Like a band of brigands," Jayne agreed, "Like small boys who've been breaking windows and stealing apples."

"More likely somebody's chickens," Amanda, ever the detective, offered. She looked ready to leap out, line them up and jot down their names and addresses.

"You haven't seen the half of the local brigands," Mags said as they took off again, "We get bears coming down to raid the garbage bins and at the end of summer you can't get a wink of sleep when the elk start trumpeting. That's their mating season when all the young studs gather to fight over the ladies. People drive for miles just to sit and watch the show. Quite something it is."

Rachel laughed: "Nice thought having all the young studs fighting over you."

"Just around the next bend," Amanda said, turning left.

The old homestead stood in a clearing, overlooking Estes Park. Amanda honked the horn and her mother came from the magnificent dark-wood log cabin – a real, genuine, no kidding Western log cabin - wiping her hands on a green rag-cloth. It reminded Jayne of another timber house she had visited.

Mags hopped from the truck before it had stopped and ran to her mother for a happy embrace and brought her back to meet the guests.

Helen Carrington was a tall, striking redhead in her middle fifties. She was, the girls would discover later, a distinguished artist. Sculptures she had made from wood and stones she collected in the mountains were placed around the big stone patio. One depicted a group of circled, dancing children made from logs, their branches the outstretched arms.

"Well, you're both welcome. Such a pity it's under such unhappy circumstances. I'm sure, though, it'll all be cleared up soon. We know of Wendy Brewer," she pointed through the trees to a white-washed house across the valley, "she worked for the Dubette family who own just about everything around here. That house is where Delta Dubette and her husband Jackson Wellman live. I've been to some of their parties … a bit too High Society for my taste."

Amanda laughed and hugged her: "Oh Mum, Delta organised that exhibition for you in Denver. You owe her that at least."

"Well, OK," her mother smiled.

She took them into the house. It was warmed by a crackling, spitting, sweet-smelling log fire in a big, open grate fashioned from rocks. More sculptures were set around the large lounge and Native American art hung on the walls. The inside walls had been left in their original state as roughly-cut half logs, now softened by a light, warm varnish and, around the fireplace, blackened by smoke.

"I've put you together in the downstairs bedroom, the windows open onto the patio. It's through here," she took them past the kitchen, where they could detect the inviting smells of a cooking meal, through to the bedroom.

There were two large beds, covered with brightly-patterned Indian blankets. More artwork, some of it watercolour mountain scenes by Mrs Carrington herself, hung on the wooden walls. Through the window they could see all the way down to the town.

"Now, make yourselves at home while I go finish the dinner. I expect you could eat something. The bathroom is through that door there and I've left you lots of towels and things. And if you need any clothes cleaned just bundle them up and I'll do them later, then Mags can show you the rest of the house. I do hope you'll be comfortable."

When she left the girls hugged one another.

Showered, changed and freshened, they were taken on a quick tour of the house. A log cabin it might be but Rachel could have fitted her Belfast apartment into the lounge alone and still had room for expansion.

Upstairs was a large bedroom facing the valley and two only slightly smaller rooms facing the mountain at the back. A bathroom lay between the front and back bedrooms.

"Dinner's almost ready," Amanda called from the bottom of the stairs.

"We'll explore outside after we eat," Mags said as they tumbled down the stairs, "We can take a walk around town."

After a great meal Rachel and Jayne offered to do the dishes but they were shooed out to the patio with Amanda and Mags where a big blue enamel pot of coffee and five mugs were already waiting. They settled around the square, plank table to savour the afternoon warmth.

"What's going to happen now?" Jayne asked Amanda.

"Well, first thing I have to do is drive into town and tell the Chief what's happened. I've assured that Captain back in Denver that you two aren't going to do a runner to the Mexican border so the fact that you're staying here counts as reporting in to the Estes Park PD.

"I guess we're in the hands of Denver. We'll just have to wait until they clear the matter up. It's just a coincidence that Wendy Brewer got the Bedroom you were originally given. Once that's confirmed you're on your way to California, though you'll have to re-book new sleepers."

Rachel looked around her: "I think it's going to be hard leaving here."

"I know what you mean," Mags agreed, "It's why I get home as often as I can."

"We were born here," Amanda took up the story, pouring them another round of coffee, "The cabin's been in the family for years, since gandfather Henry's time. It goes back to the 1880s, it was built as a vacation home by a family who made a packet from the silver mines, they're dotted all across the Rockies. When the husband died Henry bought it ... would you believe it, for something like $6,000?

"Father, that's our Dad, was a Maths professor in the University of Colorado in Boulder ... he died of a heart attack 10 years ago. But Mum always loved the cabin and was beginning to get a reputation with her art, so she stayed on. She's something of a local celebrity around here."

They said their friend Sandi, a brilliant silversmith in Belfast, would adore it here and absolutely love their mother.

Jayne told them about her New England experience and about the Schooner Cove house.

"Let's hope that's the end of your adventures," Amanda said, "You've just started your trip and you've had a big romance and a murder ... you should have plenty to write about for your newspaper, Rachel."

"Where to begin," Rachel said.

"Do you think we might need a lawyer?" Jayne asked Amanda.

"Shouldn't think so. I know that's what you see on all the TV shows – 'I want a lawyer' – but unless, and I'd say it's highly unlikely, Denver do anything I'd just sit it out."

"She's only looking for an excuse to talk to the hunky Boston Legal Brad," Rachel said.

"Well, of course you must," Mags said, "Use our telephone anytime you like. You do have his number?"

"And his inside-leg measurement," Rachel said.

Amanda got up: "I'm afraid duty calls. I'm going into the office to tell them about my two fugitives. I think it might be a good move if you tagged along, show your faces. Then Mags can give you the Estes Walk, you'll adore the town."

"OK," said Jayne, "You ready for your mug shot, Rach?"

They piled into the pick-up and drove into town, with no coyotes to give them the hard stare.

Two pretty Irish lasses with quaint accents – fugitives notwithstanding – were a big hit in the station, where every other police officer, including Detective Manuel Garcia, swore they had Irish relatives. They also all suggested that Amanda wasn't the right person for them to report to, each of them was. They were about to work out a schedule when Amanda and Mags rescued the laughing girls.

"Don't mind that lot," Mags said as she led them to the front door, "They're like a dog chasing a car, wouldn't know what to do if they caught it."

For the rest of the afternoon, she said, they'd do Estes Park and tomorrow she'd treat them to a visit to the town's most famous building: the Stanley Hotel. She pointed to it just beyond the town.

"I think I've heard of it," Rachel said,

The Stanley - designated on the National Registry of Historic Places -is one of a handful of great American hotels, beautiful and historic places full of romance and intrigue. From the Grand on Mackinac Island in Lake Huron to the New York Plaza, from the Brown Palace in Denver to the St Francis in San Fransisco and the Del Coronado in San Diego Bay to the Charleston Place in South Carolina they all hold rich strands of the country in their guilded arms. And in such exalted company stands the Stanley in Estes Park.

It was built in the neoclassical Georgian style by F.O. Stanley in the early 1900's. He had arrived in the town on board his famous Stanley Steamer car to discover that while the setting was breathtaking the amenities were sadly lacking. He set out to do something about it and purchased 160 acres from Lord Dunraven, starting work on the main building in 1907.

Not only did Stanley build his hotel, he transformed the local economy and laid the foundations of a thriving vacation spot. He also re-established a good deal of the native flora and fauna.

Where Rachel remembered the Stanley from was the classic Jack Nicholson film The Shining, whose author Stephen King wrote part of his chilling novel in the hotel, in Room 217.

And like almost every famous hotel it has its ghosts. The Stanley more than most: Room 418 is one of the most spooked among the 138 rooms and suites, with stunning views of the Rockies, Long Peak and the quaintly-named Lumpy Mountain. It even boasts an entire floor – the fourth, originally the servant's quarters – said to be haunted by children playing. And since he loved the place so much F.O. himself and his wife Flora have been seen, he playing the piano in the music room and playing billiards and gliding about the lobby.

More than enough in the white-painted Stanley for a special feature for Rachel.

They strolled through Estes Park, stopping to explore the small art and craft shops, the boutiques, the book shops, stopping in a Western shop to try on Stetsons and feathered head-dresses, to be introduced to friends of the Carringtons and to slurp an ice cream on a veranda overlooking the river.

Late in the afternoon they were found by Amanda on a second round of exploring and taken, reluctantly, back to the cabin.

As Rachel, Jayne and Mags sprawled contentedly in the chairs circled around the fire they suddenly realised just what sort of day it had been: a long train trip, a mysterious murder, questioned by the police, under suspicion, flight to the heart of the Rockies, sanctuary in a genuine log cabin, wildlife encounters with three coyotes, window shopping ... so what, Rachel wondered, will they do tomorrow?

Jayne called Brad in Boston and rejoined the group with a red-faced smile. She did say he had agreed with Amanda that they should simply wait it out, though in the meantime he would get in touch with a law firm he knew in Denver - since he was a corporate lawyer and not a criminal one – and see what they could find out about the investigation.

NINETEEN

MARVIN'S atrocious navigation had taken him off the main drag onto a series of increasingly twisting and narrow roads leading to places with those outlandish cowboy names he expected: Mesa Canyon, Dry Gulch Driveway, Dead Man's Folly. One-horse places where driftwood tumbled along dusty streets. He half-expected a band of yelling Indians to swoop from the hill and sort him out.

It did not help his foul mood that whoever was tasked with sign-posting the roads appeared to have either run out of signs to post or the will to continue. He would hang a left where the sign indicated Boulder, drive for mile after mile along some forsaken canyon and then come across a sign pointing back along the road he had just endured ... to Boulder. Either that or the last sign to Boulder he had passed appeared to be just that: the last sign to Boulder. Now he seemed to be heading for some place called Poison Springs. Bet that attracted thousands of eager tourists. Still, he consoled himself, the Indians hadn't yet managed to cut him off at the pass.

Ahead, promised another bloody sign, lay Stagecoach Halt Junction. It did not surprise him, they still probably ran stagecoaches out here. He travelled the seven miles to where the dump was supposed to be and found absolutely nothing but more trees, more crumbling bloody mountains and more dust drifting from the roadside and clogging his windows with a fine brown powder.

And what was it with all the trees? Seen one fucking tree, seen them all. Out here there were millions of them, alongside the road, up the hills, everybloodywhere. And the sky was filled with big black birds who seemed to be biding their time until he expired and they could come and pick at his lifeless eyes.

Marvin was not enjoying the scenic route to Estes Park.

But suddenly there it was: the WELCOME TO ESTES PARK carved into a roadside slab of granite. Of course, as yet it was only a sign, there was, as yet, no actual town, no skyscrapers that he could detect, no throb and hum of traffic. Manhattan it wasn't.

But suddenly he found himself driving along a street of shops and restaurants with what appeared to be real human-beings and he figured he had finally arrived. Even in his foul mood he conceded with as little grace as he cared to give that it was a nice place. Still in the middle of nowhere, but nice.

He saw what he took to be a post office and pulled up in front. He got out of the car and went through a couple of stretching exercises to force the stiffness from his back and knees. He went into the building and found a rack of tourist brochures inviting him to walk, ride, hike and ski in the 'Magnificent Mountains' – he ungraciously declined – and one for the Stanley Hotel: A Colorado Tradition Since 1909. He went back out to the car and sat in the front with the door open to consider awarding the hotel with his patronage. It looked passable.

He saw a tall, rangy guy striding towards him and asked the way to the Stanley. The man looked suitably surprised that anybody should have to ask such a question, that there was some strange person in town, obviously just arrived from a distant planet, who did not know where the Stanley Hotel was.

He pointed along the street, flapped his hand a couple of times to the right, a couple to the left and said that it was a big white building and that the grumpy-looking visitor from the distant planet really couldn't miss it.

As Marvin pulled away from the sidewalk he glanced in his rear view mirror and saw the tall, rangy guy talk to another tall, rangy guy, both of them sneaking glances at him and shaking their heads with the wonderment of actually meeting somebody who did not know where the Stanley Hotel was. They would dine out on the story until the snows of winter fluttered down over the mountains.

Marvin certainly had not expected to find such an impressive place in the middle of nowhere. He had expected to find maybe a wig-wam or a prospector's lean-to … but, OK, damn it, he was impressed as he found somewhere to park and walked to the entrance.

In his room he wallowed in a scalding hot bath and turned his mind to the solving of his problem … after he treated himself to half of a well-grilled cow and a couple of gallons of whatever cold, soft drink the restaurant could muster up.

The foul mood still lingered but he was letting it thrash through its death throes. In the morning he would feel a lot better, and in the morning he would find Rachel Andrews.

The girls relaxed in the cabin over a couple of bottles of wine, listening to stories about the Rockies told by Mrs Carrington and throwing in plenty about their lives and work back in Belfast, which Rachel wondered if they would ever see again.

Jayne was encouraged to give up more details about her New England episode and Brad and East Bayport and how, in some ways, it was so like Estes Park: beautiful and friendly.

Mags listened with amused attention to the stories and wondered why she had ended up crunching dull numbers in a Chicago office. Steaming in Summer and freezing in Winter in the Windy City did not seem to have brought her a rich store of campfire tales. Not for the first time she thought she would just stay in Estes Park, maybe find a firm downtown where she could crunch numbers. She assumed such a place existed.

Maybe she would just stay and do what she and her mother had often talked about doing: open a gallery of their own for her mother's work.

Amanda added some stories about keeping the law in Estes Park, which seemed to involve nothing more lethal than keeping the odd rowdy tourist off the booze and on the straight and narrow and chasing the odd out-of-season hunter. The occasional domestic spat. The lifestyle, she said, suited her just fine.

She had a sort-of main squeeze, one of the detectives she worked with, but it wasn't serious enough for anybody to be thinking of a new hat.

The conversation turned to Wendy Brewer and what went on at the Dubette-Wellman house across the valley: lots of parties, but nothing to get the EPPD riled up.

For some time there had been, so Helen said, rumours about an affair between Wendy and Jackson but such rumours were usually spread by the people who knew the least. He would have been a damn fool if the rumours were true since Octagon Enterprises was mainly owned by Delta and a handful of useless hangers-on and n'er-do-well family members. Jackson held only a handful of shares.

She recounted some of the more lurid legends concerning 'Bull' Dubette who had been quite a colourful character back in the day.

Helen had known Delta since they were both little girls, albeit ones who occupied vastly different worlds. She actually liked Delta, she said, and, yes, she acknowledged that Delta had been kind enough to organise a very useful exhibition in a Denver gallery. Helen had received rave reviews in the Post and the sadly now-defunct Rocky Mountain News and a slew of magazines, a couple of local radio and television slots. Delta had even paid for a colour catalogue and advertising hand-outs. So, all-in-all, she couldn't find a bad word to say about her.

She told them about the parties she had attended at The Hall, about the star-studded social line-up of Senators, writers and Hollywood celebrities, many of whom had come to the exhibition and purchased pieces.

Brad called to say he had asked his Denver friend to keep an eye on things but there was nothing new to report. He missed Jayne and was now certain he had fall …

It was well past 1am when they retired.

Still stiff from his journey, it was 9.15 when Marvin came to life. He found the local telephone directory in a bedside drawer and leafed through it, looking for the Carringtons.

There were two listings. One was for three females – a Helen, Amanda and a Margaret (no males he noted with interest) – and one for a Carrington Studio-Gallery. Both numbers covered the same address: Three Pine Ridge Park. He got out of bed and searched through his pockets for the guide-book he had picked up at the post office.

He remembered it contained a street map of Estes Park, not that there were many streets to chart. He found Pine Ridge Park which seemed, if his atrocious navigation had not broken down completely, to lie on the opposite side of the valley. It seemed to run, a faint black line, up into the mountain where it then simply petered out. He was in a room at the front of the hotel so he went to the window and pulled open the curtains to see if he could place it. He couldn't so he dressed and went in search of breakfast.

Amanda left early for work and to assure her colleagues the fugitives were still under lock and key. She telephoned Denver and told them all was well, no tunnels were being dug. Denver was still putting the pieces together but reckoned things would be sorted out in a couple of days time.

In the morning Rachel sat outside and sent articles on the Lake Shore Limited trip to the News Letter, on the Zephyr run to Denver – wisely asking if anything had turned up on the wires regarding a mysterious death on the train, though omitting, for the time being, what had happened to her and Jayne – and a couple of short travel pieces on Chicago and Estes Park. She even got a call through to the BBC, who called back and put her on the Alan Simpson show.

She figured that until she and Jayne were released by the Denver police and sent on their innocent way she was better saying nothing.

The News Desk replied that a story had been wired but since it was "just another murder in America" they hadn't bothered running it. She decided to leave it at that.

Jayne thought she had better give Brad another call, just in case. The others looked at one another and smiled. She need not have bothered for Brad said he was just about to call her. It took 25 minutes for Jayne to find out that there was nothing to report.

After lunch Helen said she was taking the pick-up into the mountains to look for suitable wood and stones for her work and would they like to join her. They eagerly agreed.

They drove through valleys and canyons of breathtaking splendour, past a small blue lake and high into the mountains above the tree line to where the terrain became almost a desert of red-brown earth. Along the way they stopped to help Helen gather twisted, gnarled wood and stones and carry them back to be placed in the back of the truck. The girls wondered what the collection would eventually become in the hands of the artist.

They had packed several flasks of coffee and a hamper of roast chicken legs, thick sandwiches and cookies and they lined themselves along the top of a mountain ridge and gazed at the winding ribbon of river far below.

Even though the sky above them was cloudless and lit by a big yellow sun, the air was chill – before leaving Helen had distributed chunky woollen sweaters – but they hardly noticed it as they sat enchanted by a view that required no comment upon it.

They continued in a wide circle around the mountains and towards early evening were back at the cabin putting their trophies in a large shed.

Mags suggested that after they freshened up and changed they could go and see around the Stanley, stop for a drink, chat to a friendly ghost.

"There might even be an Irish ghost you could interview," Jayne suggested to Rachel, "Best bring your notebook and a pen."

Helen had been, she claimed, inspired by the day's trip and decided to stay home and work on some ideas. Really, she knew the girls would enjoy themselves without her.

They headed along Macgregor Avenue and allowed Jayne to believe that it had probably been built by great-uncle Hamish. The hotel was along Steamer Parkway to their right – at the aptly-named Wonderview – and inside, in the polished wood panel lobby, they found a gleaming old Stanley Steamer guarded by a large portrait of F.O. himself, who was probably off somewhere for a game of billiards or a tinkle on the piano.

They walked through the hotel, poking their heads into the Cascades Restaurant and Steamers Café and settled at a table on the grand veranda. It was still warm enough to sit outside and hot, sweet coffee kept what chill there might be at bay.

They watched the elegant guests drifting out to the other tables.

Marvin was getting used to the high life – both in its style and the fact that the hotel stood at an elevation of some 7,000 feet – as he sat in the Cascades and finished his meal with a brandy.

Rachel went inside to get them drinks and as she was talking to the waitress she had a Keanu Reeves moment … she thought, even as she dismissed the thought as preposterous, she recognised the man walking towards the stairs, thought she had seen him somewhere before. She shrugged the uneasy feeling away, but it lingered like a small, gray cloud over her head as she returned to Mags and Jayne.

She sat in troubled silence, her brows knitted as she tried to squash the growing concern she was feeling.

"Are you OK?" Mags said, noticing Rachel's silence and frown, "You haven't bumped into old F.O.?"

Rachel did not hear her and Mags snuck a look across the table at Jayne.

"Rachel … Earth to Rachel," Jayne said, leaning over to touch her friend's arm.

Rachel came to life with a sudden shudder.

"What?" she said, "Oh, sorry … it's just …"

"It's just what?" Mags asked.

"No," Rachel said, "Just me, forget it."

The waitress bringing the drinks thankfully interrupted her, but when they were alone again Jayne returned to it.

"Rachel, something's up: what is it?"

Rachel took a long sip of her drink and gathered her thoughts.

"It's nothing, but I just saw a man and I can't shake off the feeling that I've seen him before, somewhere. It must be the thin air is getting in somewhere, I'm just being silly."

"Where do you think you've seen him before?" Mags asked.

"Is he a hunk?" Jayne asked.

"No, I don't know," Rachel said, "He's just a man ... the sort of everyday man you keep thinking you've seen before."

"It's all very mysterious," Jayne said, "Was he inside the hotel?"

"What? Oh, yes he was in the lobby, coming from the restaurant I think. The thing is I know I've seen him before, I just know it ... but I don't know where it was."

Mags lifted her bag and took out a small digital camera. She grabbed Rachel and stood up.

"Come on, let's go follow this mysterious figure. I'll try and grab a quick pic," she hauled Rachel out of her seat and ushered her inside. Jayne stayed to look after their things.

Mags and Rachel crept into the lobby and hid behind a pillar to scan the hotel entrance. Spies like us.

"Do you see him?" she asked as Rachel's gaze swept the lobby.

She shook her head: "No, he's not there ... wait a minute, that's him coming down the stairs ... who is he?"

Mags pulled her back behind the pillar and focussed the camera as their quarry reached the bottom of the stairs, clicking off three quick pics. They made their way back to Jayne.

"Was he there?" she asked.

Rachel nodded as Mags held up the camera and winked.

They finished their visit in good spirits – no pun intended – and returned to the cabin, Rachel having put the man to the back of her mind.

When they got back Amanda was there. They discussed Rachel's curious incident of the man in the Stanley and the detective sensed that the reporter was still troubled by the encounter. So much seemed to have been happening to her lately that it might simply be of no consequence ... then again it might not.

"If you see somebody you can't place but still have the feeling that you've seen them before the thing to do is try to find out who they actually are … sometimes having a name can trigger the memory of where you heard that name before," she said.

"We have the photographs, that might help us discover who he is," Mags reminded them. She showed Amanda the camera.

"OK," her sister said, "If you like I can take these into the office and start searching for a positive identity. You'll then at least know that you have, or haven't, seen him before. Won't do any harm."

Rachel agreed. She was now completely convinced she had seen him before.

Rachel and Jayne accompanied Amanda back to the police station early the following morning, with the camera. Amanda introduced them and explained to an intrigued colleague what they wanted and he immediately set to work with his computers.

"It really is like CSU, isn't it?" Rachel whispered to Jayne as they watched the photographs whizzing through the screen.

"Nothing on the local database," the colleague said, sliding his chair around to face them and leaning back with his hands locked behind his head, "Short of taking the photos to the hotel and asking who the man is …"

"Don't think that would be a good idea," Amanda said.

"I agree," her colleague nodded, "If he is somebody Rachel has seen before it might be something she wouldn't want to repeat, and if he's just an innocent tourist we wouldn't want to embarrass him."

Rachel nodded.

"Anyway, we haven't exhausted all of our options here," the colleague unlocked his hands and swung back to the computer, clicking it into another database, "You might like to leave this with me, I'll go through as many possibilities as I can but it will take some time."

"I have some reports to catch up on and I'll give Denver another call," Amanda said, "Why don't you two take a walk, have a coffee and come back in, say, a couple of hours?

"And don't worry, we'll get to the bottom of your mystery. You've been under a lot of stress, I'm so sorry your trip has turned out like this."

They walked into the town and stopped at a riverside café for coffee and Danish, sitting outside at a table.

"You still think you have seen him before, don't you?" Jayne said.

"Yes, and I'm damned if I can recall where. It's really bugging me," Rachel said.

The time dragged but they eventually returned to look over the shoulder of Amanda's colleague who was still tapping frantically at his keyboard.

He stopped and turned to them: "I've tried every database I can get into and I've even sent the photos to Denver, State, the FBI, CIA, military and Homeland Security to see if they can pin-point your man ... the only people I haven't yet tried are the Boy Scouts of America. They're all going to get back to me, but I doubt if they'll put a priority on it. Sorry, I'm clean out of ideas."

They thanked him and went to find Amanda. She was sitting at her desk surrounded by a pile of files and papers. There was still no news from Denver.

She walked them to the door and then had a thought: "You should try to remember where you think you saw him, however unlikely it might seem."

Rachel agreed to try it. She and Jayne retraced their steps back into town, found another café and had another coffee.

"OK, let's give Amanda's idea a try," Rachel said.

Jayne started her off: "So would it have been in, say, Belfast? Maybe you saw him on the 'plane to New York, in New York itself? Was he on the train, either of the trains you've been on?"

Rachel thought: "I don't think I saw him on the Limited or the Zephyr, no I'm certain I didn't. Nor on the 'plane .... I saw so many people in New York I can't think ... "

She ran his image through her brain, watching it flash through like the police computer.

"In Belfast," she said suddenly, "Belfast ... I think I saw him in Belfast, and just recently. I did see him in Belfast," she gave it more thought, "and in New York, at the hotel. He was sitting in the lobby of my hotel."

She was now fired up: "Let's get back to Amanda, I think we have a way of pinning him down."

They ran back to the station to see Amanda, still working through her papers.

"I'm a bloody nuisance," Rachel said, "But I think I've seen him in Belfast and in New York. Can you send the photographs to my newspaper in Belfast, I'll give you the number and e-mail address, and could I telephone a colleague to look out for the pics?"

Amanda directed her to an empty desk and Rachel made her

call to Brian Leonard.

When he came on she barely gave him time to say "Hi!" but went straight into an explanation.

"I'm in a place called Estes Park, in the police station – no, don't ask, just listen carefully – and I'm getting them to send you a couple of photographs, OK?

"So – look, just listen – could you get them to Detective Inspector McMurtry and see if he's ever seen the man before. It's important, of course it's important, I wouldn't be calling you from Colorado – just listen – if it wasn't.

"I need to get this man's name and to find out if he has ever been in Belfast …"

Brian obviously managed to stop her for Rachel fell silent, nodding furiously. Then she broke in: "I think I saw him in Belfast just before I left for the States, but I don't know who he is … it's important you find out. Can you see McMurtry as quickly as you can?

"You can contact me at … hold on," she turned and raised her eyebrows at Amanda who scribbled down the PD and cabin numbers for Rachel to read out, "Got that, Brian? Good, I'll explain later. Don't hang about."

She put the 'phone down and slumped over it. Then she picked it up again and punched in the News Letter number.

"You're still there, Brian; why are you still there? OK, just remembered something else might be important: I think I saw him around the time Meredith Harling disappeared. I don't know what that means: nothing, something, everything. I think it's important."

She turned to Amanda and gave her a short synopsis of the Meredith Harling story: the Tabernacle, the big opening, the discovered scam of the American backers, the missing millions, how she and Brian had covered every aspect of the story.

"And you think this man has something to do with all that?" Amanda asked.

"I don't know, but if I'm right he was in Belfast when Meredith went missing. That's too much of a coincidence, don't you think?"

Amanda considered it for a moment then said: "I'm beginning to think it could be even worse than that. I'm thinking it has something to do with the Wendy Brewer murder … and, I'm afraid to say, with you. Maybe you are, indirectly and innocently, involved in the case … maybe you switching sleepers on the Zephyr had a bearing on what happened."

"My God!" Jayne's hand went to her throat, "You think this man was targeting Rachel, that he didn't know it wasn't Rachel in that Bedroom?"

Amanda made a pushing down movement with her hands: "Let's keep calm, we're only making wild guesses ..."

"And scaring the wits out of me," Rachel added.

"Sorry, but you're right, that's the last thing I want to do. Let's not get ahead of ourselves. We'll wait until your friend comes back with more details. Who's this McCartney he's going to see?"

"McMurtry," Rachel said, "He's John McMurtry and he was the PSNI cop who investigated the Harling case. He became a good friend of Brian and me. If anybody can help us in Belfast, McMurtry can."

"OK, so we're agreed: no panic moves until we hear from Belfast."

They nodded their agreement.

In the News Letter Brian sat back in his chair and wondered what the hell Rachel had got herself into now, she couldn't cross an empty room without the ceiling caving in on her, it was trouble that was warned not to go looking for her, it would only get trouble into trouble.

A girl – new girl, he noted – approached his desk and handed him two photographs. He studied them: some dude standing in what looked like an old Scottish baronial hall, all big chairs and potted ferns, dark wood panelling and a log fire. One of the photographs was clearer than the other, it was the one he would get to McMurtry, if he could track the policeman down.

He reached for the telephone on his desk and fished through the papers to find his contact book. He flicked the pages to McMurtry's number and punched it in.

It took some time for the policeman to come to the 'phone. Brian reminded him who he was and asked if he could come see him, he added that it had something to do with Rachel. He wouldn't swear on it but he thought he heard a low groan.

The policeman told him he could spare a few moments around 4pm, so long as the reporter made it a few moments, like straight in, natter-natter, straight out. OK!

Brian said that's all it would take but knew that McMurtry wasn't buying it.

It was 3.30. Brian finished the story he was working on and

grabbed the photograph. He walked briskly down May Street to meet the policeman.

They sat in what looked to Brian to be an interview room – dull gray metal table, a couple of uncomfortable metal chairs, a tin waste-basket overflowing with plastic cups and scrunched pieces of paper – as he told McMurtry what he knew, which was precious little.

He slid the photograph across the table. He asked if the policeman recognised the man.

McMurtry gave him the cold stare: "I'm the one who usually asks questions like that in here."

He toyed with the picture then shook his head: "Not off hand."

He flipped it around in his hands some more: "You say Miss Andrews had it sent from the police in this Estes Park place? What's it supposed to mean to us?"

Brian felt slightly foolish since he really hadn't a clue, Rachel never gave him time to pick up any useful additional information.

"All I know is that she thinks she saw him in Belfast around the time Meredith Harling went missing … and that photo was taken yesterday in Estes Park. She also has this weird notion that she also saw the guy while she was in New York. I know, it doesn't make much sense to me."

He was sharp enough to realise he had grabbed McMurtry's undivided attention by mentioning Meredith Harling.

"So she thinks this guy is connected to the missing Harling woman?"

Brian shrugged: he still hadn't a clue: "She didn't say that, not exactly."

McMurtry pushed his chair back from the table and stood up: "OK, leave this with me. Don't know where I could begin but I have a couple of names from the Harling thing, one of the Trustees, actually it's the one who first got us interested in what was happening. I have a number, think I'll run the pic under his nose. I'll get back to you … and remember the usual: not a bloody sentence in the 'paper."

Back at his desk, Brian took the second photograph from his drawer and looked at it. It was a less defined shot of the man in the hall-lobby-whatever. He tapped it on the desk, thinking. He thought he had a lead. He went in search of the picture library.

The news of Jackson Wellman's departure from Octagon Enterprises shocked Denver, the news of it was everywhere and not just in the Business sections. It made front page news, was lead item on most of the radio and television casts and was even played up as a stunner in the Wall Street Journal.

Delta brought her closest ladies-who-lunch friends together at The Hall and gave them the barest of details: marital difficulties, trial separation, still friends … life goes on, have another G&T.

Since Jackson appeared to have vanished from the face of the Earth, life did indeed go on, with Delta now firmly in the driving seat.

TWENTY

McMURTRY drove up the Newtownards Road for his meeting with Harold McKillen, or the Tabernacle Man, as he thought of him. As he threaded his way through the traffic flowing out of town, the policeman pondered the afternoon's developments.

There were still so many loose ends untied when it came to the case of the previous year: the Tabernacle scam, the murder of Max Harling, the disappearance of Meredith Harling, the missing money, the connection at the time with American funding, what the present connection might be and how it was linked with the man in the photograph.

It had been one hell of a headline-grabber at the time: the mind-boggling plans Harling had for the building of a zillion-pound Tabernacle on the south side of Belfast – the auditorium for thousands, the film studio, the radio and television and video complex, the publishing house, and don't even get into the media circus that was the ground-breaking ceremony – and his death, followed by the discovery of Meredith's murky past in the States, followed by the discovery of the skimmed-off millions, followed by a wild dash to a small Greek island, followed by a boat chase that ended in an explosion, followed by the death of Coren Armstrong who had been dating Rachel Andrews.

He shook his head at the sheer soap opera scale of the bloody thing. And now, out of the blue, was the opera going into another act? So was the man in Estes Park the key to it all?

McMurtry turned right at the lights into Sandown Road and checked the address he had been given, it was at the far end of the street on the left.

He sat in the front room overlooking a flower-filled garden while the Tabernacle Man scrutinised the photograph.

"It's the best they could do," McMurtry explained, "But if you can think back to the ..."

The Tabernacle Man looked up at him: "I'd much rather forget it. But ..." he returned to the photograph, "all I can say is that if this man's now in America and if he was in Belfast then he must have been with the Yanks who put up part – a good part – of Max's funding. He must have been a very silent partner because, honestly, he made absolutely no impression on me ... the only impression they made as a group was that I thought they'd all stepped out of a Godfather film."

McMurtry nodded, then added: "Miss Andrews, Rachel Andrews the News Letter reporter who covered the, er, the thing back then, took the pic yesterday in America and she's pretty sure she saw our man in Belfast a couple of weeks ago, around the time Meredith disappeared. Jog anything?"

The Tabernacle Man shook his head and handed over the photograph: "No, nothing. Sorry."

In the News Letter Brian was following exactly the same line. He was scrolling through the newspaper's photo archive to the used and unused picture coverage of the ground-breaking ceremony. He might just come across a mug-shot of Rachel's subject.

A lot of photographs had been taken, not all of them ending up in print and, he knew, not all of them kept on file. Chances were, he guessed, any pics with the man on them had long been binned.

He rolled the screen quickly through the archive for the big day itself but nothing screamed boo and leaped out at him. He went back several days before the ceremony, with the same results, and several days after it, same results. He returned to the day itself and studied each photo more carefully, enlarging the group- and crowd-scene ones with particular interest.

Local celebs and politicos beamed back at him, sober-suited men and flower-dressed women stood in stiff clusters for one uninspiring photo after another. There were a couple of small, one-, two-, three-strong groups pictured with Meredith, looking like the sexy fashion plate she was back then. But still the man eluded him.

He went for a stimulating coffee, brought it back to the computer and tried again ... back and forth, up and down, from right to left and back again.

Just as he was about to abandon the job as a lost cause, and after scrolling past it several times, he found it: a group photograph with

Max and Meredith and four sharp-suited men. And at the back of the group, looking like somebody who did not want to be photographed and was about to hurl himself on the photographer and smash the camera, stood the mystery man.

Brian compared the group picture with the one he had kept from Rachel. It was a difficult ask but the more he flicked from one photograph to the other the more he was convinced: it was the man.

Which, unfortunately, was all he had for there was no caption to identify any of the people other than 'a group taken at the ceremony' … obviously the photo had never been used in the 'paper's extensive coverage of the Tabernacle opening.

To make sure he was not mistaken, to assure himself that he had not picked on this particular photo because he was getting tired and desperate to find the man, Brian did another careful comparison.

He made a note of the photograph's number and where he could find it again in the archive. He sat back, rubbing his tired eyes back into focus. So, he thought, Rachel had been right: her Estes Park man had been in Belfast back then and might possibly have been in Belfast just recently and might possibly have had some connection with the disappearance of Meredith Harling. Certainly, the man knew Meredith, he had evidence of them having been together. He wasn't sure what it all meant but he figured McMurtry would find his discovery of interest.

Brian left a note for the photographers to run off a print and planned to get it into the hands of McMurtry first thing the following morning. Before he left the office he sent an e-mail to Rachel bringing her up to date on the day's progress.

He was first into the office the next day, though overnight a thoughtful photographer had printed up the picture he had asked for. He owed his colleague a swift half. He gave the photograph one more test and in the cold light of morning still thought there was a strong likeness.

He found McMurtry at his desk when he called just after 9am, explaining about his search through the archives and about his find. The policeman was very interested.

Brian offered to bring it immediately since McMurtry said he was anxious to show it to McKillen, his Tabernacle Man.

"He works in the Bank of Ireland in town," he told Brian, "Maybe seeing your man with the Harling couple will jog his memory. What we need is a damn name."

The policeman and Brian arranged to meet for a coffee at 11am, by which time he might have made some more progress.

They met in the Arizona Expresso in Chichester Street.

"We're in luck," McMurtry said with satisfaction, "My man thinks this guy," he tapped the group photograph, "was one of the Americans who funded the Tabernacle, or at least he was with them. McKillen recalls that he didn't say much, always seemed to be lurking in the background.

"Anyway, McKillen thinks his name was Demme. If Miss Andrews thinks she saw him here just a couple of weeks ago I'll assume he arrived from the States and I'll assume it was either into London or Dublin. I'll ask the Southern lads to check it out and I'll get Scotland Yard to see if they can trace him through Heathrow or Gatwick. Though with our luck he'll probably have rowed over from bloody France. Still, it's worth a try."

"What do you reckon it all means?" Brian asked.

McMurtry shook his head: "I'm not sure. Look at it this way: this guy was at the Tabernacle do last year, Miss Andrews thinks she saw him around the time Meredith Harling went missing, then she thinks she saw him in New York and then she takes a snap of him in this Estes Park place … whatever it means I don't care for it much.

"My guess, and a wild one it sounds, is that the Americans are still looking for their money, that's got something to do with Meredith's vanishing, and they might think Miss Andrews knows something about it. Did she ever talk to you about it?"

"No," Brian said after giving it some thought, "Rachel had a pretty hard time after Coren was killed. Maybe the Americans think he told her about the missing millions, but I honestly doubt it: he kept quite a lot from her."

McMurtry finished his coffee and got up: "OK, I'll start the wheels turning … oh, and don't forget: not a word of this in the News Letter."

TWENTY-ONE

STILL feeling like they were being held prisoner – though in wonderful circumstances – Rachel and Jayne decided to make the most of their unscheduled stay in Estes Park with the Carringtons.

Their plans to reach San Diego were now in tatters, though Rachel had still not plucked up the courage to tell the newspaper, and there was still no word from the Denver PD that they could try to put them back together again.

They did go to Denver with Mags in the pick-up but just to take a look around the city, do some retail therapy, try to get their minds off their dilemma. As a courtesy, on the suggestion of Amanda, they did call into the local police to assure them they had not sneaked off. It seemed to satisfy the DPD who told them that events were moving to a conclusion, a vague but somehow comforting statement.

They tramped around Larimer Square, the historic old district of Denver, and visited almost all of the intriguing shops. They visited the State Capitol, dropped into a museum and watched a presentational video about the history of the city, had a meal in a fancy restaurant … and even paid a somewhat chilling visit to gaze at the Octagon Enterprises building.

They played at being the perfect sightseers and enjoyed every exhausting minute of it.

The following day Amanda joined them for a trip to one of the abandoned silver mining towns and a trip into a freezing cold mine shaft to learn that many of the miners had actually come from Cornwall. They bought lots of silver bracelets and necklaces for Sandi.

They visited exotically-named places like Deadhorse Mill and explored deserted towns that had once boasted ornate opera houses and several newspapers and had been thronged by rowdy hell-raising miners until the silver ran out. They watched daring white water rafters battle the churning, boiling rivers.

It would, Rachel consoled herself, make for a great feature. Mags and Amanda were making a great job of entertaining their unexpected guests and taking their minds off the reason for their stay.

Back at the cabin their marathon trips were topped by Helen's great cooking and a relaxing slump out on the patio, with glasses of wine and conversation.

Marvin, on the other hand, was feeling anything but relaxed. He had watched Rachel from as safe a distance as he could but somehow could not find her alone long enough to act. She was always with one or several of the women, or visiting the local cops or taking off somewhere in the pick-up. He had followed and saw more mountains, trees and crumbling old buildings than he cared to.

Amanda had grabbed some of the days off she was owed and one morning as they sat outside over breakfast she suggested they might like a hike – nothing too strenuous, she assured them – up the mountain that lay along the path behind the cabin.

Jayne excused herself because she had to get her Coast-to-Coast notes together … more like Coast-to-The-Middle notes. More likely to call Brad in Boston, Rachel said.

Mags also had to turn down the hike since she was due to return to Chicago the following morning.

Helen had gone into Estes Park to meet some friends and plan a possible exhibition in one of the galleries.

Rachel, however, agreed and Amanda took her inside to sort out a pair of suitable, comfortable boots and something more fitting than a whispy nightdress or a fashionable pair of expensive jeans. What was required, Amanda said as she looked through the wardrobe, was a pair of stout, baggy canvas trousers, a couple of thick shirts and a heavy sweatshirt, chunky woollen socks and the suitable boots.

Rachel, looking like a miner who had strayed into town with his honking mule, posed for a photograph when she was presented to the others.

"My God," said Jayne, "It's Gabby Hayes!"

Marvin crept through the trees towards the cabin. He had driven his car from the hotel anticipating another jaunt around the Colorado scenery but when the pick-up failed to appear with Rachel on board – it did pass but there was only one person in it, the older woman of the group – he had decided to take a closer look. He had parked his car well off the main road in a copse of trees at the corner of the cabin's dirt-track.

At first he did not recognise Rachel, all he saw was somebody dressed like a mall garbage-bin scavenger posing while one of the others took photographs.

Everybody seemed to be having a jolly time. The jolly times were about to end, he thought to himself, ducking back into the thick bushes to watch the activity.

By now he had figured the scavenger was Rachel since he recognised the cop and the two other girls. He watched as the cop and Rachel moved off along the path beyond the cabin and keeping to the trees on a parallel path he took off after them.

They walked side-by-side, stopping occasionally to look down on the river winding towards the town, pointing out whatever caught their eye.

The path they were on was steep and in the trees it was dangerously slippery from riverlets of water seeping down the mountain, crumbling where the earth had dried out in the summer heat.

Branches reached out to snag him and he almost gave himself away when his foot caught in a gnarled root. He scrabbled up, keeping the girls in sight over to his right, pulling himself along by the branches.

They had stopped again and he watched the cop point up ahead. He heard, between the creaking, rustling trees, rushing, tumbling water and scrambled ahead to where a waterfall cascaded over a craggy ridge and fell into a bubbling pool, the mist from the 'fall drifting through the trees. From the pool the water found an escape through a narrow channel and tumbled along a rocky stream.

He rested against a tree and wiped the spray from his face as he waited for the girls to catch up. They stood at the edge of the pool and looked down at the foaming bubbles.

"There's a fairly easy path above the 'fall over to our left," he heard the cop say.

"Shit!" he said, realising they were now coming in his direction. He scrambled further into the trees, certain the noise would be detected. It wasn't. They found the easy path and bent into their climb, disappearing from his view as the trees grew thicker.

He ducked and weaved, keeping them to his right – or where he hoped they still were – and finally spotted them up ahead.

Around him he could hear the mysterious sounds of the forest and guessed they had assumed his dash to safety was merely nature rampant. He had the feeling he would suddenly find himself confronting a hungry bear or a pack of wolves looking for an afternoon snack.

The girls stopped again as Rachel bent to fluff up a purple flowered bush so Marvin took the opportunity to rest. At least, he figured, there were only two of them, which put the odds a little more in his favour. If he could only get the Andrews dame on her own.

He felt in his jacket pocket. He had brought a gun but figured it would not be too wise to use it. A shot, however successful, would waken the neighbourhood and have him hunted through the bloody woods like a mad, foam-flecked mutt. Anyway, he didn't want the reporter dead – well, not just yet – he wanted to grab her, get her down the mountain and into his car … for a little chat.

As the girls took off again he pushed himself up, his slipping feet sending an avalanche of stones bouncing and pinging off the trees.

Then he saw his chance. Rachel had wandered off from the cop and was moving towards him. He could still see the cop off to the right, slowly picking her way carefully up through a dip in the mountain. He flattened himself against a tree and waited for Rachel to pass him.

She did, but she was too far away for him to risk a quick dash from his hiding place. She walked off through the trees and he heard the cop calling to her.

"I'm over here, Amanda," Rachel called back, "Over to your left, there's a small clearing here."

Amanda, that was the cop's name, he remembered now.

"OK," Amanda called, "I know it, don't move. I'm coming over."

He heard the cop pushing through the trees. It was time to reduce the odds to even, one-on-one. Get rid of the cop and leave Andrews stranded in the trees and vulnerable.

Still listening for the cop and trying to figure how far away she was, he searched around for a makeshift weapon. He found a thick moss-covered branch and tested it in his hands.

Amanda walked right past him and he stepped from behind the tree and swung the branch. He heard the crunch as it connected with the back of her head. She fell to her knees, trying to gain a foothold, trying to force herself upright. He stood over her waiting for her next move but she turned to face him, groaned softly and sprawled out. He poked her with a foot and her lifeless body slid and tumbled down through the trees until it disappeared below him.

"Amanda, you still there?" Rachel called.

No, baby, Amanda ain't here any more, it's just you and me ... and I'm coming. Marvin used the branch to steady himself as he moved towards Rachel's voice and the clearing. Just you and me.

Rachel was still calling to Amanda, directing her to the clearing. Marvin skirted to his right where the trees offered more protection, keeping Rachel to his left until he could pin-point where exactly she was standing in the clearing.

"Shout all you like," he muttered, crouching low as the trees began to thin out towards a small circle of fallen, charred trunks, "She ain't gonna come."

He bent low and worked his way behind her. A twig snapping under his foot reverberated through the trees and Rachel turned sharply towards him.

"Amanda, I'm ..."

Marvin stood, the branch in his outstretched hands like a hitter ready for a sure-thing home run, and charged into the clearing. Rachel stood waiting, a look of fear and sudden recognition on her face. She tried to move, tried to get her feet to sort themselves out for flight but they would not co-operate.

He was upon her before she realised it. He swung the branch and she yelled as a searing pain shot through her shoulder, spinning her around to canon off a tree. She staggered backwards and stumbled to her knees. He hit her again but by now she had gathered some momentum, falling and pushing herself upright, clawing at the earth for a strong grip.

She saw a chance to get out of the clearing when he swung and caught an overhead branch with a shuddering thwack. He cursed and chased after her as she made for the safety of the trees.

Tears filled her eyes, blinding her to where she might escape. She wiped the back of her grazed and bleeding hands across her eyes and crashed through the forest back to where she had last seen Amanda.

She slid and tumbled down as the ground beneath her gave way, rolling and pitching like a ball down a rocky gully and to a thud against a tree, the breath forced from her aching lungs with an animal-like whoosh. He was still coming after her, still waving the branch about his head.

197

Rachel looked frantically around, trying to remember the direction she had taken to the clearing. From below her she heard the roar of the waterfall and made for it, her legs buckling and her shoulder throbbing with pain.

She found the ridge and ran towards the cloud of spray she could see through the trees.

She could hear Marvin panting and wheezing close behind her, every step carrying him closer. She was losing the strength to continue, waves of sickness brought the bitter taste of rising bile to her throat. She threw up as she ran, the vile-smelling vomit pouring from her nose and mouth, spraying her face and splattering over her shirt.

Marvin had stopped briefly, listening and bent double to pump air into his lungs. He watched as she ran along the edge of the ridge towards the path beside the 'fall. He followed, gaining ground in the desperate race.

As Rachel made the river where it gathered speed for its dive over the ridge and into the pool below, she turned and began sliding and bouncing down the path. Marvin stopped at the 'fall and aimed the branch down towards her, jumping after it as it turned slowly and arced towards her.

The branch hit her below the knees and she crumpled, reaching out for anything that would stop her fall. Branches shredded through her stinging hands but didn't stop her plunge.

She struck the rim of the pool and somersaulted forwards, head first into the cold water.

She splashed in panic as she felt her legs being grasped by the grass and dead branches deep under water, pulling her under. She kicked out and surged into the centre of the pool. She was freezing in the water but found the strength to flail out and claw her way to the far bank.

Marvin reached the pool and watched her scrabble in the wet poolside earth for a way out. He ran around the pool, staggering into the river but forcing himself on.

Rachel was sprawled on her stomach, retching up lungfuls of water, her heart thumping in her chest. He kicked her over onto her back and grabbed her hair to drag her back to the pool.

He thrust her head under until she stopped struggling and clawing at his arms, until the bubbles stopped foaming from her nose. He pulled her up and she fought for breath. He pushed her back into the water.

Rachel felt herself losing the will and the ability to save herself. She had no strength left, she was going to die. She could no longer keep the water from sluicing through her teeth and down her throat. She felt a blackness creep through her.

She did not know how long he had held her under but she felt herself being dragged from the water. She lashed out, kicking wildly with a strength and fury she found somewhere deep inside ... and passed out.

Amanda regained consciousness, somehow. She was wrapped around a tree trunk and her head throbbed. She lifted a hand and carefully felt the back of her head, groaning as her fingers found the open wound. Her hand was covered in blood and glancing down she saw that blood had seeped down her neck and over her shirt. She gulped in air and levered herself to her feet. She took a tentative step forward and fell to her knees in the damp moss, the bile spewing from her mouth.

She tried again and this time managed to stay on her feet, looking around her to figure out where she was. She had tumbled down through the trees and was somewhere near the waterfall. She could hear it nearby.

She tumbled through the trees towards the sound and came crashing through to the pool Just ahead of her, his back turned, she saw a man standing over Rachel. Instinctively she grabbed a rock and aimed it at the back of his head. She heard the crack as it bounced off his skull. He turned in surprise, made towards her. She hit him again and he crumpled to his knees.

She ran to him and dragged him by his hair to the nearest tree.

Rachel was following a light along a long, shimmering tunnel. She thought she could hear, far off somewhere, birds singing, trees rustling in a warm breeze. At the end of the tunnel she exploded into daylight. Above her she saw thick white clouds playing hide-and-seek with the sun.

She turned and raised herself on her side, vomiting and spitting water.

Beside her lay Amanda, her breathing shallow but steady. Rachel lay in silence and tried to gather her thoughts. She rolled over to Amanda and lifted her head. Blood was seeping from a deep gash, trickling through her fingers. She shook her friend and called her name. Amanda slowly opened her eyes and smiled.

"Oh my God," Rachel said, "you look awful … and your head …"

Amanda felt her throbbing head and winced at the blood on her fingers.

"And you look even worse," she said, reaching out to Rachel, "What the hell happened?"

Rachel suddenly remembered and jolted upright: "That man … in the photo … the one … he …"

"Oh yes," Amanda groaned and pointed, "He's safe, whoever the hell he is."

Marvin was slumped against a tree, blood seeped from an ugly red gash on his head.

"Is he dead?" Rachel asked.

"No, at least I don't think so … the bastard deserves to be, though. He hit me and I must have passed out. When I came too I heard you yelling and saw him standing over you with a rock."

"Bloody hell!"

"So I found a bigger rock," Amanda said matter-of-fact, "and hit him with it. Years of playing softball with the local lads finally paid off."

She tried to stand up but a wave of dizziness swept over her. She sat down, and threw up.

"I think I can make it," Rachel said, pulling herself up, "Will you be OK? Will you be safe with him? I'll go get us some help."

She steadied herself on wobbly legs.

"Just make it quick, my head hurts like hell. He won't move, I've tied him to the tree."

Rachel went to take a look and saw that Marvin's hands had been secured around the tree with Amanda's jeans.

"Get back to the cabin and gets the girls to call the police."

Rachel coughed up the last dregs of the pool and looked at her friend.

"Don't worry, as soon as I mention that you're up here in your underwear they'll all come running."

"So make sure the girls get here first … with a pair of jeans. Now get going."

Amanda watched as Rachel staggered groggily off down the path. She felt the back of her head throbbing with a dull pain. She peeled off her shirt and pulled herself to the pool. She dipped the shirt into the water and squeezed it into a ball that she held to her head. The sudden coldness helped ease the pain.

Across from her Marvin groaned and stirred and began struggling to free himself. She picked up a large rock and rolled over to him, shoving the rock into his face.

"Listen to me, you miserable son of a bitch," she said, "One more twitch from you and you get this, understand?"

Marvin nodded.

As Amanda scrambled away from him he snarled after her: "Fucking cow!"

She rested against a boulder and smiled at him.

Rachel, falling and sliding, finally made the track and headed for the cabin, crashing through the front door and collapsing.

"Rachel!" Jayne called, jumping from the desk to her friend, "What happened?"

The noise brought Mags from upstairs and together they helped Rachel to the sofa, plumping cushions for her head.

Rachel explained what had happened and Mags grabbed the telephone to call the police.

Rachel, still soaked from her plunge into the pool, was shivering, her teeth rattling. Mags went to the bathroom while Jayne pulled the clothes off Rachel. They wrapped her in a warm, fluffy towel and rubbed heat back into her. They washed her torn and bleeding hands and knees.

"The boys in the station are on their way," Mags assured her, "And they've contacted the para-medical team. They'll have Amanda soon."

TWENTY-TWO

CAPTAIN John Brand of the Denver PD was holding court. He sat in a blue chair in the room Rachel and Amanda had been sharing for the past two days in the Estes Park Medical Center. Jayne and Mags sat on each of the beds and Helen Carrington fussed about the room trying to find space for another bunch of flowers.

"It isn't like you see on television," the Captain was saying, "It isn't all neatly wrapped up in an hour, the Judge doesn't break down and confess his guilt to Perry Mason ..."

The patients nodded, wondering where exactly the monologue was going.

"Anyway, we're getting the full story from our guest," he went on, "And, boy, has he been doing some travelling."

The details had come from Brian and McMurtry in Belfast, from all across the USA and from the Estes Park PD ... they made for a twisted and complex tale.

McMurtry and the PSNI, working on Brian's discovery of the photograph in the News Letter, had traced Marvin through Heathrow, using his United Kingdom passport in the name of Martin Demme, the name McKillen had remembered.

McMurtry had sent all of this information, plus Marvin having been in Northern Ireland at the time Meredith Harling went missing, to the Denver PD.

They, in turn, found out that a Martin Demme had booked a coach seat on the same California Zephyr that Rachel and Jayne had been travelling on. So far, he had not admitted murdering Wendy Brewer but the girls' altered sleeper arrangements clearly suggested that he had ... by not knowing that Rachel was no longer in Bedroom 11, Coach F.

Additionally, a thorough search through several data banks

linked a Martin Demme and a Marvin Gerstein with a series of mysterious Cold Case killings in a string of cities across the USA and Canada.

And Amanda had won a clutch of Brownie Points for the Estes Park PD by bringing him in. And, of course, Rachel and Jayne were free to resume their journey, once the doctors gave the all clear.

Several days later, with the all clear having been declared, the girls sat on the patio of the cabin soaking up the hot, refreshing sunshine. Rachel and Jayne had tried to get re-booked on the Zephyr to California but no sleepers were available since it was booked solid until the middle of August.

Somehow, though neither said so, they were not too disappointed. Helen had told them they could stay for as long as they wanted. Mags had reluctantly returned to Chicago – vowing to give serious consideration to coming back to Estes Park to open that gallery – and Mrs Carrington welcomed the company.

Rachel wrote up the story for the News Letter: another EXCLUSIVE with Brian Leonard that rounded off the long-running saga of the Harlings.

Jayne sent Brad a copy of the story and arranged to meet up with him when he returned to Ireland in early September.

At The Hall, Delta read the reports of Marvin's arrest for the alleged murder of Wendy Brewer in the Post and smiled slyly. She had completely re-structured the management of Octagon Enterprises. There was even a 'new' Jackson Wellman she had her eye on. She was, alas, not able to attend the funeral of Miss Brewer, but would always remember her.

ENDS

Breinigsville, PA USA
03 December 2009
228595BV00004B/9/P